PRACTICAL HYPNOTISM

Author
Dr. Narayan Dutt Shrimali
M.A., Ph.D.

V&S PUBLISHERS

Published by:

V&S PUBLISHERS

F-2/16, Ansari Road, Daryaganj, New Delhi-110002
☎ 011-23240026, 011-23240027 • *Fax:* 011-23240028
Email: info@vspublishers.com • *Website:* www.vspublishers.com

Branch : Hyderabad
5-1-707/1, Brij Bhawan (Beside Central Bank of India Lane)
Bank Street, Koti, Hyderabad - 500 095
☎ 040-24737290
E-mail: vspublishershyd@gmail.com

Branch Office Mumbai
Jaywant Industrial Estate, 2nd Floor–222, Tardeo Road
Opposite Sobo Central Mall, Mumbai – 400 034
☎ 022-23510736
E-mail: vspublishersmum@gmail.com

Follow us on:

For any assistance sms **VSPUB** to **56161**
All books available at **www.vspublishers.com**

© **Copyright:** *V&S* PUBLISHERS
ISBN 978-93-813844-6-6
Edition 2015

Printed at : Param Offseters, Okhla, New Delhi-110020

Contents

PUBLISHER'S NOTE

The science of hypnotism basically belongs to one's soul. Modern researches have revealed that man's soul can be divided into two parts—internal and external. A hypnotist can only be successful if both these parts of the soul get united. The book contains the process of uniting these both parts of the soul according to the Indian Tradition.

It is absolutely necessary to keep the soul clean from any stains so that our society and country may progress properly and the social values may get re-established once again. But this needs a very strong will-power, which can be taken care of by the science of hypnotism. In view of all that, hypnotism has become more important and useful in the modern context.

The writer of this book is an acclaimed intellectual, who has helped the modern Indian society in many ways through his writings. This book does not merely contain the gist from other books but it has the author's reflective as well as analytical thinking with which every reader can benefit and learn the science of hypnotising. Besides the main hypnotising principles from the West, the book contains the Indian thoughts and principles too on hypnotism, as well as the ancient ways and procedures of meditation. The reader will surely be benefited by all that.

The incidents and happenings listed in the book are based on the author's imagination. Therefore, neither he nor the publisher will be responsible for any untold happenings connected with those events.

MOST REVEREND
DR. NARAYAN DUTT SHRIMALI

Human life and the universe are full of known and unknown mysteries. Man is always tempted to rediscover the known mysteries but when he tries to find out the facts about the unknown, many new things come into light.

As the civilization is advancing rapidly, discovering things related to the unknown have become a happy practice. In fact, human journey has taken a great stride starting with the invention of the wheel until the creation of the computer.

As a consequence to the latest technological developments human life has become much easier and happier but at the same time it (life) is also exposed to insecurity, fear, disappointments, sleeplessness and fear of another war. Can that be considered a real development in civilization? Our Old Rishis had rightly said:

Let all be happy and prosperous.
There should be no misery to anyone.

Then where has the above precept disappeared? Why are people unhappy? Why is man not contented and does not get satisfaction and fulfilment? Our Vedic culture was always implicit with scientists like Sushrat, Aryabhatta and Bhaskaracharya. Besides, the great risk is like Sankaracharya, Gautama, Vishwamitra, Vashishtha, Atraya, Kanada & Ved Vyasa have been great thinkers, who discovered the principles of life. Their main contribution was to discover how a man can travel free of any ailment on the journey of life from birth until death. Their discourses gave birth to *Mantras* as well as *Tantras* causing to discover the necessary devices that would help in completing the tantric activities. Yoga system was actually developed to bring unity between the dvine and the man. The Rishis believed that the universe possessed unlimited energy and man could get it unceasingly with the help of Yoga and redeem himself from ailments. That belief consequently originated the idea of gods and goddesses, hypnotism, *sadhana*, Science, *mantra*, yagya, and such activities.

Dr. Narayan Dutt Shrimali who donned a new name after renunciation, resolved to spread the knowledge of hypnotism to all. To fulfil it he travelled throughout the country. Though he led a life of a saint, he believed in the *grahastha* too. The books he wrote contain the ideas that can lead anyone away from *sorrow to* happiness and contentment. Thus, he wrote books on *mantrasastra, tantra-sastra,* hypnotism, astrology, palmistry and *ayurveda* and gave them all a scientific temper.

During his 65 years of life he contributed a lot towards knowledge because he believed that knowledge is permanent. He also started publishing. In 1981 he published a monthly journal named *MantraTantra-Yantra Vigyan,* through which he clarified many mystic ideas and beliefs. It has helped millions of people to uplift their lives and to live peacefully and happily. He left for heavenly abode on the 3rd of July, 1998 when most of his work to enlighten people was over. It is worth mentioning here that his monthly journals, *Mantra-Tantra-Yantra Vigyan* and *International Siddashram Sadhak Pariwar* are still widely circulated. It is a testimony that he always believed that ideal knowledge is permanent and that it can help people to attain emancipation.

—Nand Kishore Shrimali

INTRODUCTION

In India hypnotism or the art and science of hypnotism, to be precise, has been a priceless asset. It has been sanctified by timeless traditions. It was largely from India that the rest of the world learnt and followed and imbibed this knowledge. Evidently the outstanding achievements recorded in India in this discipline has remained unsurpassed by and large.

India, at this stage, is passing through a strange crisis, beset as it is with a harrowing sense of uncertainty, a self-defeating apathy and a turbulence which has overtaken its teeming millions. A haunting sense of insecurity appears to have taken the people of India in its vicious grip. Look at anything whatsoever and you will feel terribly put off by the very brokenness or lack of integrity or sheer incompleteness of things. The kind of society such as we have envisioned to have, eludes us, the structures having gone awry and the fabric grievously missing.

What, one fears, principally accounts for this frightening confusion is the Western impact on India. For the Indian mode of life has always been contemplative and inwardly, the *summum bonum* of which was an intuitive grasp of the truth. As part of such contemplation the Indian endeavour has been to delve deep into the dark recesses of the inner self and realise all potential existing in any form and to any degree whatsoever. No wonder the ancient seers of India chose to overlook the empirical dimensions of the material world and preferred as such to retreat into solitude. Through contemplation they always tried to envision, comprehend and identify the human form gifted to mankind by the Almighty, and discover the potential of the powers that lay embedded in the human body. They contemplated the elements which brought off the human body in its form. They made a total submission to the Almighty, and went deep into these profound mysteries and elements so that man derived a great measure of happiness and higher powers, and extended his environment to a yet wider canvas.

Conversely, the West remained riveted to the external world. Seldom did it try to seek out answers to the complex questions of body and soul. The West hardly bothered to know how body and soul came into being, and what all we could do to extend the frontiers of human environment. Instead it remained bogged down merely in the external trappings of customs, modes of living, eating habits and culture and civilization. The West was merely interested in exhibiting its deeds. It was more interested in showing off its superiority. The Western idea, unmistakably, was that man is what he himself wills to be. Understandably, man, as the argument runs, owes nothing whatsoever to the powers beyond, to the Creator, the *Brahma* and to the immanent power of soul.

It was precisely for this understanding that the West tried to enrich only the external trappings of the human body. Obsessed as it was with only physical comforts and leisurely life, the West brought into existence a whole body of science as also a series of inventions. The exercise led only to the tilting of the sensualness of the human flesh.

Needless to say the outcome of the Western obsession led to a precipitate shrinking of man's wider canvas. When he found himself reduced to narrower concerns, the Western man set out to dominate others, approves the weaker sections and seek fulfilment in founding and extending imperialist empires. Soon, however, he had had good cause to realise that this entire exercise—the manner as well as the object—ended up in utter futility. For he found that despite possession of empires and extension of materialistic claptrap spiritual peace continued to elude him.

Extending the horizons of science did not ensure any spiritual peace, and without obtaining internal bliss it was futile to pursue any other object. The vast empire, the army of retainers, the comforts and the treasures—each one of these was an exercise in futility, for peace—the peace that passeth understanding—withdrew to a yet distant goal. Indeed the more one chased the sciences, the more one found exposed to lack of inner solitude.

Eventually as West turned its attention to India, it found in this country, startlingly, a society not rich by Western standards and yet distinguished by an innate tranquility. Also a yet remarkable feature of this society as the Western quest found out was its achieved sense of self-fulfilment. When men from West advanced into the dark, thick foliage of the Indian forests and saw there scantily clad *Sadhus*[1] who, surely, did not have any material possessions, not to speak of opulence and yet sparkled with a radiance of their own, they wondered what, after all, was that power which secured them such profound self-fulfilment and such remarkable achievement.

It was this discovery which made West turn its attention to East, particularly India. Men from West arrived in this country and set themselves to go deeper into the factors and mysteries which ensured India its fulfilment. They also began to explore the reasons which gave India its inner strength and a pivotal position in the comity of nations, although the people were not at all rich by any material standards.

Now, for the first time, people from the rest of the world realised that peace and tranquility do not stem from the showy outward trappings of civilization. Nor can one have it from high concentration of brutal strength in any form whatsoever. Peace and tranquility do accrue, but only as part of the imperceptible process of contemplation which must, necessarily, involve an identity of the elements accounting for the physical and spiritual dimensions of man.

It was in contemplation of the Indian achievement that the West, for the first time, discovered that the human body has as its basic structure a crucial element which is mind transcending the frontiers of time and space. In other words, the fact that man is endowed with superior powers can only be attributed to the position that he has in his mind which governs human physique. It is by virtue of this faculty that man laughs, cries, feels and expresses his joy and also gives a shape to such

---

1. *Sadhus:* Saffron-robed mendicants, a characteristic feature of the Indian spiritual life.

speculations as are not at all rooted in the present. The West which basically believes in materialism sought to locate where and in which part of the human body the element known as mind or the complex known as psyche was rooted. For this reason scholars of the West drew heavily upon anatomy and dissected the human body to locate, in physical terms, the lodging place of the mind. The object of such scholars was to get hold of the mind. Once they thought they would get hold of it they could hasten its development and succeed in delving deep into the recesses of the soul. However, despite all dissections and investigations, they failed to come across the exact location of the mind. Now they failed to identify even a single complex which resembled the mind or psyche in any form or manner.

But in any case the West felt bound to accept the view that the mind remained embedded in the human body. For it was the mind or psyche which governed the functioning of the human body. The entire human body was subordinate to the dictates of the mind. It was by and large the mind which makes man laugh and cry, resent and rejoice and help develop these manifold faculties.

It was only after obtaining this realisation that men from West, for the first time, veered around to the view that the mind was second only to the Almighty. Besides, its peculiar importance stems from the fact that the mind paves the path to reach Godhood, not to speak of the astounding mysteries which have remained unravelled. Science might take centuries to reach the fountainsource of all these mysteries. On the contrary, the Indian seers have already unravelled the knots of all the mysteries and have largely identified the factors which make our life as comfortable as it has come to be.

Indeed the power inherent in the mind power is that it can make possible what looks like impossible. Its speed is unrivalled in that it transcends all dimensions of time and space.

As the seers and godmen tried to explore the element known as mind or psyche, they were pleasantly surprised to discover that the mind consisted of two segments—the outer mind and the inner mind.

Every minute the outer mind sees, and records our responses to, the physical world and the physical phenomena. At times when it is rendered inactive, for instance, when man falls asleep, the outer mind is left with no particular job. Needless to say while asleep with eyes closed, the outer mind is not exposed to any physical phenomenon outside.

At a time when the outer mind is rendered inactive, the inner mind springs into brisk activity. Being active it reaches the higher planes of consciousness and seeks to see such phenomena which it had never seen before. More often than not, it sees even such incidents or phenomena as had never taken place. This state of being is called dream.

In this manner, man sees through his inner self even future events. It does not entail any difficulty for the inner mind to retreat into the past or peep into the future. At times he views even such events as had never materialised before. When, however, at a future point he finds the same dream sequence materialising in real life, his surprise knows no bounds.

Once in a dream Abraham Lincoln, the U.S. President, saw that he had been murdered and that his dead body was lying in the White House. The deadbody was covered with a piece of white cloth, and his wife and other members of his family, were mourning his death. In the dream he had seen the assassin and noted that he emerged from a certain room of the White House. He stopped at a certain place, and then advanced to murder Lincoln who died instantaneously.

The horrid dream woke him up. He found himself sweating all over the body. However, he took care to make a minute recording of the dream sequence in his personal diary. He also took care to inform his wife the details of the hideous dream. He gave her the date and time of the dream-murder.

It was indeed astounding that Lincoln was murdered in the same manner on the same date and at the same time as he had seen in the dream.

That dreams come true at a future point has been the experience of many persons. This, at any rate, is nothing but the activity of the inner self which actively, emerges on the scene when the outer mind is rendered dormant, and looks beyond into the future. The indication, unmistakably, is that the inner mind is capable of peeping into the future. However, since we do not have full control over the inner self we do not always see in our dreams such incidents as we would like to see at a given time. When, for instance, we want to know the exact place, date and manner of somebody's death, we would foresee the event long before it actually takes place after exercising full control over the inner mind.

It was only when this insight was obtained that the Western psychologists mounted deeper investigations into the inner mind. Hypnotism or Mesmerism codifies investigations and related facts of this nature.

Accordingly, they found that the mind has two entities—the outer mind and the inner mind. The outer mind is more active and it records whatever man does or sees. It is also called memory. It is by virtue of this faculty that one remembers things long consigned to the past.

For instance, he remembers when he married—and who he married and who all attended the marriage. At the time of marriage his outer mind remained active and it recorded the event. The record remained for many years, and whenever he sought to recall the past event, he remembers it. The scene of the event revivifies before him.

In any case the outer mind records the moments of the present. It does not have any capability to go into the past or peep into the future. The inner self does have the capability to do so.

It is only by developing the inner self that one can have the success one longs to have It is, therefore, essential that the inner mind is made stronger and healthier so that it works at a greater speed. In that case one can make it do any job one assigns it or show any scene one likes to see.

The mind gives rise to a multiplicity of ideas. Since man basically is a slave to desires, he has various kinds of desires crowding about. He works hard to fulfil the desires. Suppose he wants to build a house. He will need money for this purpose. This will entail him in incessant efforts to earn money by means, fair or foul.

A single desire leads to many subordinate desires. For instance, the single desire is to raise a house. It will touch off many subordinate desires such as collecting and hoarding money and take measures of security and what not. The desires involve man in all kinds of activities. Some of these desires get fulfilled, while others do not. The fulfilled desires make him happy, while the unfulfilled ones drive him mad.

When the mind is cluttered with all kinds of desires, man desperately tries to advance each desire to its goal. Often the outcome is that his endeavour gets fragmented and his energy and capability fail. The inner mind loses its speed and man loses control over the inner mind.

The scientists found a way out. They recommended a sharp decrease in the number of desires. It would, they argued, bring about a corresponding lessening in the stress accummulating in the mind. It would stem the charge on its energy. It would also ensure a more effective functioning of the mind. In that case, the mind will not only peep into the future of the subject but also foretell the future of any other person.

To describe this state Indian seers have used the expression—the mind free from ideas. For instance, let us drive out all ideas and desires from our mind. A mind devoid of ideas and desires is an unalloyed mind. It is only a mind of such accomplishment that can secure us fulfilment of our desire. For there would be no other contending desire to detract the attention of the mind. Should we, for instance, ask the unalloyed mind to tell us what is in store for us in the coming ten days, it will certainly foretell us giving a graphic description of the events likely to take place in the coming ten days. It does so, for the mind is not cluttered with ideas or desires. Nor has it lost its speed. Neither has its energy expended extravagantly. It will respond to what we suggest.

To make the mind unalloyed is not that easy. It involves certain methods and certain techniques. It is only through this medium one can have a mind free from ideas or desires.

First of all, we must have the bare minimum of desires. Besides, our mode of living should be simple and unpretentious.

Secondly, we should focus attention on our inner self. Calm and collected we should sit at a quiet place, close our eyes and internalise our whole being. We should dissociate ourselves from the external environment. As we do so we shall be descending into the innermost recesses of our inner self. It will give us an internal light and we will see the unlit corners of our inner personality. Initially it will be a frustrating exercise but gradually we will overcome the difficulty. We will succeed in achieving concentration on one single object.

Tratak is about the only simple method to achieve a total concentration in contemplation. It ensures a one-point concentration, casting away all other ideas or desires as we go deeper into meditation. In the process all mental activity gets concentrated at one-point in *Tratak* giving us a mind free from ideas or desires.

Although palmistry and astrology can also reveal the past and the future, these sciences are not complete in themselves. There is yet much scope for research in these sciences. Unless these sciences emerge as complete in themselves we cannot hope to make an integral study in either case. But long before any of these sciences hypnotism has already achieved the proven capacity to know the past and the future. By knowing the past and the future we are in a better position to shape our present life. Indeed this achievement must go down as the highest watermark in the spiritual explorations of mankind.

I personally feel every person should practise *Kriya Yoga*. It alone would ensure a tension free life. Anybody can practise it, but one needs a teacher. It will not be possible to effectively handle *Kriya Yoga* without a teacher. Sex, age, colour—nothing stands in its way. The method is so simple that one can master it only after a few days' practice. Even the busiest person can be benefited if he practises it regularly in morning and night. He will feel cheerful and happy.

True in the initial stages he might feel slightly put off, for despite his repeated attempts he fails to bring about concentration of mind. When he sits for this exercise with his eyes closed, a crowd of dissimilar ideas disrupts his concentration. The best and simplest way to achieve concentration is *tratak* which has been discussed in this volume in some detail. When the person succeeds in concentrating his meditation he has to internalise it with the aid of a special technique. It exercises a check on the wayward mind. The technique which brings about this check and helps internalise the meditation is known as *Divya Sadhana*[1]. This *Sadhana* is popular mostly among the *Yogis*. It lightens the body and helps gain control over self.

To get through the austere practice of the *Divya Sadhana* one must take to regular practice of certain special *yogas*[2] and *asanas*[3]. There are eight *asanas* and one must practise these in a certain order. This helps achieve what is known as *Divya Sadhana*.

It is only by a sound mastery over *Divya Sadhana* that one develops the strength to go deeper into, and help identify, his inner self.

Soon, with the aid of *Divya Sadhana,* he tries to obtain an idea free outer mind. Gradually he begins to feel quieter and also lighter. But one confronts difficulty when the outer mind has to link up with the inner mind. For both are separate entities and in no way reciprocally related. It is only by virtue of a special technique that the outer mind establishes a link-up with the inner mind. Once the link is established it is imperative that the unity remains unimpaired.

When the link is established and is also related to the special technique the process of obtaining an idea-free mind begins. What is catalytic to this process is the impact received from the outer mind. No doubt the process is somewhat difficult,

---

1. *Divya Sadhana: A sadhana* having a supernal or transcendental vision.
2. *Yoga:* Hindu system of philosophic meditation and asceticism designed to effect the reunion of the devotee's soul with the universal spirit.
3. *Asana:* A posture of sitting, and the exercises prescribed.

but once we gain control over the outer mind, it would not be difficult to bring the inner mind under control.

When the inner mind is made devoid of ideas, it begins to link-up with the outer mind. The link-up process is known as *Kriya yoga*, which involves many other actions. It results in a rare experience of poise, happiness, desirelessness and dissociation from negative feelings such as attachment, greed, anger, hatred and the like. A state of being such as this makes a person *Sant*[1].

When man reaches such a state of being he experiences a celestial light which emanates not from any external source but from his inner self. Until then the inner mind remains clouded in the thick fog of desires. Once the desires are removed, the light comes out on its own.

It is only after achieving this celestial light must one treat his *Kriya yoga* as successful. *Dhyana yoga* begins from where *Kriya yoga* ends. Although *Dhyana yoga* is not indispensable, one must remember that *Kriya yoga* in itself is not complete. Without *Dhyana yoga* one is not expected to get the desired outcome.

When the *Sadhak*[2] plunges deep into his inner self, he sees initially a dot of light. Gradually the circumference of the lights gets bigger. One begins to see a bluish reflection of light. As we reach the innermost recesses of his inner mind, we begin to see a brilliant light and the circumference too gets widened.

After some time the bluish reflections will vanish. The light which emanates from all sides of the rounded dot assumes many colours—all seven colours. When the person has seen this multicoloured light, he may presume that he has perfected his *Dhyana yoga*.

The person should continue this practice for some time. Soon he will stop seeing the multi-coloured vision. He would straightaway see only the brilliant celestial mass of light. He would see his inner self brilliantly lit with the help of this mass. This light would not be confined to any limits.

---

1. *Sant:* Saint.
2. *Sadhak:* One who is engaged in austere worship of God.

What the *Sadhak* cannot simply overlook is that he must remain sharply conscious of his being if he wants to reach this state. He must keep on asking himself: Who am I? Why do I do this *Sadhana*? Why do I sit for the *Sadhana*? What do I want to see through this *Sadhana*? What do I want to gain out of this *Sadhana*?

When he begins to see the infinite light, the *Sadhak* will find his third eye being opened up, which will bring to his view the past and the future. It should be very easy for him to know when a particular incident took place in the past and what is going to happen in the future, and when.

In no case should this be treated as the dead-end of the *Dhyana yoga*. A little more practice or following a distinct special practice will get the *sadhak* the frontiers of the light far more extended, and the obscure corners of the many preceding lives will come out fully alive. In a perfectly chronological order the happenings of the past lives such as place and time of birth, growth and decay, quality of life and other facts of similar import will reveal themselves to the full glare of the viewer. What is more important, the knowledge garnered therefrom will also tell the *Sadhak* as to why his own thinking, his own consciousness and his own psychology in the present life is what it is.

Much in the same way the life to come after the present life will also come out alive, should he choose to see beyond. He will come out with certain knowledge about the specific date of his death as also its cause and the circumstances obtainable then. He will also see where he is going to be born in the next life, how he is going to be brought up and what events would characterise his next life.

Through *Dhyana yoga* not only the *Sadhak's* own past and future are revealed but the past and future happenings of several lives, both preceding and succeeding, of any other person can also be known, provided he meditates for some time to invoke such happenings in his daily *Dhyana yoga Sadhana*.

A regular and persistent practice will enable the *Sadhak* to know all about the past and the present in less than one hundredth of the time one normally takes reading, say, the printed line of 8 to

9 words. Significantly, when he comes out of the inner self and returns to the consciousness of his outer mind, he remembers all events and scenes, together with the time of occurrence.

1. INITIATION

Hypnotism is the oldest knowledge of India. It is rooted into the deepest traditions. A spiritual outlook has always characterised the Indian life. It was for this reason philosophy and spiritualism figured importantly in every walk of the Indian life. Hypnotism was also called *Pran*[1] *Vidya* or *Trikala*[2] *Vidya*[3] in ancient Indian literature.

After its initial phase of glory this knowledge mostly remained buried on obscurity. It was pushed into the realm of witchcraft, which always remained as the special preserve of certain families.

In the West, however, hypnotism was an object of curiosity and mystery. The people of the West had a keen inclination to investigation and research. When they learnt all about the miracles of the Indian seers, they were simply amazed. They visited India, and saw for themselves that the *yogis* could achieve the impossible. By a mere touch of their fingers, they would cure patients of their ailments, communicate knowledge about persons located far away and see anything anywhere all over the world as clearly as they saw the person sitting opposite.

Not only this, they delved deep into the past and dug out facts long embedded into the unknowable. Indeed the entire exercise stunned the people of the West, who, for the first time, found cause to realise that the knowledge beyond touch and sight was as real as the physical sciences, if not a lot more miraculous.

The human physique is a complex of certain strange and inexplicable phenomena, which have always baffled the scientists. They dissected the physique to locate its mystery. And yet they could not identify the physique in its entirety. Nonetheless they discovered in the human body such

---

1. *Pran*: Life, the first of the five vital airs or these five airs collectively.
2. *Trikala*: The past, the present and the future: these three ages collectively.
3. *Vidya*: A system of knowledge.

elements as might not be visible and yet nobody could disprove their existence. The mind, for example, is such an element. It might not be seen but nobody could disprove its existence. Anatomists dissected the body and yet they could not locate any limb known as mind. However they conceded that this part was the most crucial constituent of the body without which it would be reduced to mere bones and flesh devoid of emotions and feelings.

It should be essential to know the mind before one seeks to know all about the physique. The mind is said to be the most forceful constituent of the body. Often it has been seen that a person by virtue of the force inherent in the mind can achieve seemingly impossible things. By dint of sheer will-power and perseverance the individual succeeds in negotiating the most difficult turns in his life. Take, for example, the case of a dying man whose son is posted far away. He is determined to see his son before death. By virtue of this staying power he continues to live long enough to see his son, although the physicians had given up all hopes. It was often seen that a determined person like him managed to live on for another 3 to 4 days. The moment the son arrives, the determination disappears and the man dies the next moment. It was only on the strength of the forceful mental power that he could linger on.

No wonder Indian *yogis* spent most of their time to comprehend this elusive element—the mind. They looked within and went deeper into the inner self. The accomplishments they came out with have been the object of envy throughout the world. The Western philosophers, on the other hand, concerned themselves only with mere externals. The major thrust of their explorations was calculated to tilt the sensuousness of the physical body. Doubtless they scored some significant achievements in the realm of the physical world. As they went closer to certain accomplishments in the physical world, they found themselves, no less by the same process, far away from the essential element—the mind.

It was only when they saw Indian accomplishments and comprehended Indian methodology that the West resiled from its unproductive methodology and trained its sights on the internal world of the being. Credit must go to the renowned Swiss scientist Dr. Enton Mesmer who was the first Western thinker to have initiated studies in this methodology and brought off a scientific study of hypnotism. It was after him that this science—mesmerism—derived its name.

Dr. Mesmer was born on 23 May, 1734. Following a close study of the achievements of the Indian *yogis* he began to realise that the entire creation, both animate and inanimate, was permeated with an invisible power[1]. It was, he felt, imperative that this invisible power be identified and creatively used. For he began to see that this invisible power being ubiquitous was extraordinarily influential in respect of the animate world, and more so, in relation to man.

Every human organism, he also felt, was endowed with a magnetic power, whose presence one felt when two persons meet. The meeting draws the latent power out. He called it animal magnetism operating as it did in both negative and positive forms. In males the positive form and in females the negative form operate.

When the two forms meet each other, the resultant form grows into a full circle which is an unmistakable indicator of its full force. Take, for instance, the sudden glow in the eyes of a certain man when he chances upon a certain woman. Generally the reaction is due to a special electric current which heaves his body up and down. The positive magnet longs to meet or touch the negative magnet. It is only through this process do we obtain a full circle. As Dr. Mesmer explained, birds and animals, too, react in the same manner. Even when two positive or two negative currents meet, a particular type of magnetic power gets generated.

As Dr. Mesmer explained, the entire organism is permeated with magnetic power. When we give a hand-shake to somebody, we feel either overcome or overbearing. What accounts for this varying range of feelings is that one may have more magnetic power than the other.

---

1. *Invisible Power*: Identified by the Indian *yogis* as *Pran Shakti*. It is also known as bio-energy.

In 1775, when Dr. Mesmer first made public his findings, a great commotion overtook Europe. It was an age characterised by blind faith. While some persons commended Dr. Mesmer's findings, others pronounced it to be anti-religion and contrary to natural phenomena. The Austrian Government took it as big crime and ordered him to leave the country within 48 hours.

Exiled from Austria, Dr. Mesmer settled down in Paris where he established a regular clinic. By then he had successfully carried out many experiments and also proved that many chronic diseases could be cured with the aid of the magnetic power.

He selected a room of the clinic and magnetised its walls. The magnets affixed on the walls were invisible, and yet the room exuded an attraction of its own. Also he got a sweet-smelling scent sprayed all over the room. Barely outside the room he arranged soft music which added to the pleasant atmosphere in the room. Patients suffering from chronic diseases were made to sleep in this room. He planted a suggestion in the patients that they were recovering fast. The interaction between the magnets planted on the walls and the magnetic power inherent in the bodies of the patients gave a lot of relief to the resting patients. Besides, in the sheer delight of the room patients often enough used to forget their ailments. For medicines he gave them plain water, though bottled in attracting phials. He saw to it that all kinds of high-sounding labels were pasted on the phials so that the patients had the satisfaction of being attended to in a special manner.

The experiment cured many patients and won him popularity all over France. Many high-ranking officers and ministers visited the clinic and went back fully recovered.

While conducting these experiments, Dr. Mesmer felt that the finger-tips had in them a high concentrate of magnetic power which otherwise permeated the whole body. He also felt that his own finger-tips very often gave much relief to the patients through touch. He used to notice that the patient got a kind of relief when he touched with his finger-tips either the location of the wound or heart as the case might be.

These findings brought about a sea-change in his thinking. Now he was convinced that the animal magnetism inherent in the human body could be activated by a mere touch of the finger-tips of another body. He began to see merit in the way the Indian sages of ancient times showered blessings on the suffering persons. The practice was that the sages would touch the suffering person with their finger-tips. It was as Dr. Mesmer now began to see calculated to activate the animal magnetism in another human body. The sages would also say: You are now cured. The very suggestion brought about better feelings leading to a quicker recovery.

Dr. Mesmer also found that if a magnet was placed on a sore, the germs got destroyed. If a magnet was placed in the water of a tumbler and allowed to remain as it was for some time it would, he saw, give a startling effect to the patient.

Soon Dr. Mesmer widened the scope of his medical activities. He would make his patients squat in a circle and place at the centre a magnetic tree. He would cover the magnets under a loose shirt and himself stand close to the centre of the circle. As a result, the magnetic power would activate and strengthen the relatively weak magnets functioning in the bodies of the patients. As soon as the patients felt a redoubled supply of magnetic power in their own bodies, they would start feeling hale and hearty.

Dr. Mesmer's experiments, each one of them being resoundingly successful, soon made the physicians of France feel jealous of his success. They conspired against him. He was forced to leave France.

Dr. Mesmer's initial experiments were very successful. He cured innumerable patients of their ailments. The common man looked upon him as a magician. Gradually, the intellectuals started taking his experiments rather seriously. Some of them, who became his disciples continued the experiments, taking it to yet greater heights.

Dr. Mesmer died on 5 March, 1815. By then his experiments had roused tremendous enthusiasm all over Europe. Almost all top intellectuals and scientists like one man acclaimed that

Dr. Mesmer's experiments ensured cure for all diseases. The French Government appointed a committee of physicians and members of the French Academy of Science to submit a report on his experiments and results. The committee accepted that the principles underlying Dr. Mesmer's experiments had the potential to ensure cure, but the principles did not stand scientific tests. Accordingly, the Government did not recognise his experiments.

Dr. Mesmer's disciples further developed his experiments. Of them, Dr. Marquis Ap Piesager won wide recognition in this field. Literally he changed the very orientation of Dr. Mesmer's experiments.

Dr. Marquis developed Dr. Mesmer's hypotheses into a scientific theory. He proved that a patient could be induced to sleep through hypnotism and cured through hypnotic suggestions. He sought to achieve through hypnotic sleep what Dr. Mesmer achieved through his magnet treatment.

Physicians as well as scientists commended this theory as very objective and dependable.

With a touch of his finger-tips through which magnetic waves used to pass, Dr. Marquis used to put his patients to a particular type of sleep. Now he would conduct on them a series of experiments. The patients would not know of it. Chloroform had not been invented by then. So the surgeons faced lots of problems while working on their patients. Dr. Marquis' method coming at a time like this proved a boon to surgeons. Now surgery did not give the patients the inhuman torture it used to give.

Meanwhile a lot of work was accomplished in this field. Professor John Eliptonson, who was professor of medical science in the University of London and also president of the Royal Medical Society, applied this method on mentally deranged patients and established that if such patients, after being induced to sleep, were given a proper orientation, the chances were they would recover from their mental maladies sooner than expected.

In 1841 Dr. James Braid further developed this method. He established that the patient could be cured sooner if he was induced to hypnotic sleep and the hypnotic suggestion was implanted on him that he was recovering very fast. Even incurable disease, he showed, could be cured through hypnotic power.

Dr. Braid proved that hypnotic power was inherent in every individual. He could use this power on himself. The eyes more than any other limb, he argued, stored the hypnotic power and magnet touch. In pitch darkness, too, the eyes of the tiger or the cat poured forth powerful light. It was nothing but magnetic waves. The power was found in the eyes of all, though in varying degrees. If a person, argued Dr. Braid, had a somewhat limited magnetic power in his eyes, he could strengthen it by experiments.

He further elucidated that a person could make his mind free from thoughts by fixing his gaze at a certain point or a certain flame. As he would slowly and steadily strengthen the magnetic power of his eyes, he himself would soon fall to hypnotic sleep. No doubt he could derive for himself the benefits one normally derived from other persons under hypnotic spell.

Dr. Braid used the Greek word *hipnos* which meant 'sleep'. Now the term hypnotism replaced mesmerism. Dr. Braid's achievement received wide recognition all over the world.

Dr. Braid's work was followed up by a galaxy of scientists from various countries. Dr. El Wakeritz of the U.S., Dr. Liu Bault of France, Dr. Charcot, Dr. Nancy, Dr. Sheimound Hood and many other distinguished scientists worked hard to further develop it into a viable scientific theory. It made a tremendous impact on the treatment of the patients suffering from hysteria and other mental maladies.

Dr. Braid's findings were recognised in India too. A surgeon of Kolkata, Dr. James Esdeler made certain experiments to which he added the well-deserved component of *yoga*. He successfully conducted certain risky operations on the patients after inducting them to hypnotic sleep. He also perfected the technique of painless delivery as also painless tooth-extraction.

Dr. Charcot used the scientific form of hypnotism for certain special experiments in the field of medical treatment. He found that the female-patient experienced the same symptoms under hysterical spell as she came across during hypnotic operation. In respect of symptoms, both were, therefore, identical. He also proved that hysteria was by no means a disease. It was the sequel of one's suppressed or non-realised desires. Excessive suppression led to hysteria. If a woman, for instance, was not satisfied with her husband sexually, she was likely to contract hysteria. In the same way, a married woman suffering from childlessness might have hysterical fits, the cause being her own non-fulfilment.

The causal factor, argued Dr. Charcot, should be taken care of. The desire was the causal factor. During hypnotic sleep, the suggestion might be planted in her that she would derive full satisfaction from her husband or she would be giving birth to a child in the near future. This by itself would be a contribution to her cure. Dr. Charcot treated a number of patients by using the method of hypnotic suggestions and hypnotic sleep.

Later Sigmond Freud achieved a remarkable success in this area. He firmly established hypnotism in the field of medical treatment. He established that the sexual desire lay dormant or suppressed in every individual, whether he is a two-year old child or an eighty-year-old grandfather. He also said that what the child did when sucking at, or fondling, his mother's breasts was nothing but a form of sex fulfilment. Once the sex desire of a certain individual was sublimated, he would be cured of his malady. It was entirely a different matter as to what sort of sex desire it was and how it could be sublimated. In any case one could not, argued Freud, think of life without some form of sexual desire. Every moment of the individual was spent in sublimation of his sexual desire. It might assume any form. Waiting for the departed beloved or reflecting over the endearing moments they spent together or playing with the child—these forms were nothing but manifestations of sexual desire. Mother was terribly attached to her son while father was as much attached to his daughter—these forms were also some sort of sublimation of the sexual desires.

Sex must in any case get its expression. Otherwise it would lead to stress and all kinds of complexes. Hypnotism alone could provide relief against such maladies.

In India too much work was done in this field. The first to revive this science in modern form was Professor S.N. Bose who published a journal to spread its message to the common people. He set up a school too, where an experiment form of this science was put across.

Others who further developed this science in India include Professor Ahmed, Dr. Jagdev Mitra, Professor Rao and a few more.

Indeed the human form is simply amazing. God created this unique system in such a manner that once we comprehend the magnetic qualities and influences inherent in the body, it should not at all be difficult to make the impossible possible through this medium.

OO

2. HYPNOTIC POWER

In man a special kind of energy and magnetic power are obtainable. For instance, pull a hair off your head and secure it a location so that the wind does not sway or effect it. Now advance one of the fingers of your right hand to the direction of the hair. You will see as you bring your finger closer, the hair will move towards being drawn to your finger, much in the same manner as an iron filling does to the magnet.

When the individual contemplates, or thinks of, his beloved, a particular kind of magnetic power passes through, and heaves, his body. Often he finds vibration in his fingers. When all of a sudden the lover comes across the beloved, her face turns red, her eyes shine with a red glow and at the same time a peculiar attraction gets generated with an extraordinary power to pull others to her. It is by virtue of this magnetic power that woman attracts man. Man, too, does so with the same power. His body at that time goes particularly attractive.

Let us take a commonplace situation. When you come across a healthy person, put your finger rather earnestly on his forehead or very close to his head. Let your finger go around his head. If you ask him in a couple of minutes, he will admit to having a sort of pain in his head. The headache could be attributed to the magnetic power which shoots from your finger-tips and impinges on the head or the forehead as the case may be.

Certain human bodies contain vaster deposits of magnetic power. Resultingly such persons are more popular. It is now no more a question of debate that we are all endowed with magnetic power in varying degrees. It is by virtue of this power can one hypnotise the other person or persons.

The need today is how to increase the magnetic power potential already provided in our physiques. One must seek to increase to an optimum degree one's own magnetic power potential. One cannot hope to hypnotise others without first attending to this basic task.

All objects of the universe, whether animate or inanimate, are governed in each case by a certain gravitational pull. The male is attracted to the female of his species. It is, again, gravitational pull which controls the movements of the planets and the stars. What is known as astrology is a study in influences and counter-influences caused by planetary magnetic forces.

One comes across hypnotic power potential not only in men and women but also in birds and animals alike. The snake puts a check on the movements of its prey through a special kind of magnetic power shooting from its eyes. The python gives a piercing look to the deer standing more than 10 feet away and the poor animal finds itself totally petrified.

Hunters have often reported that the eyes of the animals which fear threat to their lives give out a particular kind of glow which is entirely different from the usual. It is, therefore, not difficult for the experienced hunter to smell the presence of a lion or tiger near about, particularly after ascertaining the scared looks of the other animals in the neighbourhood.

We have seen from experience that there are two kinds of magnetic power inherent in all living beings—the normal magnetic power varying in degree from individual to individual with which he attracts others, and secondly the magnetic power which springs into life only in anticipation of danger, which also ensures him security.

Magnetic power, I have already argued, is obtainable in each and every individual. The one who has more developed magnetic power can easily attract others, while the other, who does not have magnetic power to that degree, attracts others superficially. A bigger magnet, for instance, can easily and powerfully attract the smaller iron piece. The plain and simple reason is that the magnet being bigger contains a greater volume of magnetic power. Its atoms separately and severally are equipped with a higher density which in aggregate generate a particularly superior kind of power. As a reaction, the iron piece finds itself drawn to the magnet.

It is only rarely that we come across all human beings

equipped with such developed magnetic power. But if the atoms of the magnetic power are given a greater volume, the magnetic power will certainly increase. Equipped with such developed power one can always attract others. In other words, the individual can increase the inherent magnetic power by a set of practices.

Through experimentation, testing and practice we could, Dr. Mesmer had explained, increase our magnetic power as much as we choose to have. Besides, magnetic power, he had also explained, could be transferred from place to place or it could be made to assume a different form too.

Thousands of years ago Indian seers had proved beyond doubt what came to be suggested by Dr. Mesmer. Then it was called *Pran Shakti*. This particular kind of *Shakti* or power can tie developed through *Pranayama*[1] and a particular type of *yogic* practices.

Through *Pranayama* as we can draw into our bodies this *pran* or life power, so can we transfer it to other bodies and make them disease-free or even restore life to the dead and also increase the life span of individuals. The ancient scriptures of India testify that the *yogis* could resurrect the dead by a mere touch of their fingers. The *yogis* used to condense in themselves such a lot of *pran shakti* that they could transfuse life into the dead by a mere touch of their fingers.

The *yogis* called it Ether Power. Where there is void there the sky spreads itself. The entire universe is absorbed in the sky. It implies that ether power and life power (*pran shakti*) are basically the same. In other words, the entire universe is permeated with *Pran* or life power. In a moment, we reach all corners of the universe through the medium of this life power.

The *yogis* called this power timeless. It means that the time which has gone past can also be known with the help of this power. Even the future time can also be seen with the aid of

---

1. *Pranayama*: Breath control as prescribed in the *yoga* system. In broad outline, the process of controlling breath by inhaling through only one nostril and then stopping the breath by controlling both nostrils and, finally exhaling the breath from the other nostril.

this power. Endowed with this power, the Indian *yogis* used to see the moments of the past as well as the future in the same manner as we see the moments of the present.

The magnetic power, we have already argued, could be further developed with the help of certain particular spiritual practices. The more we develop it, the better we see the unknown places, the unknown moments and the unknown mysteries.

Dr. Jagadish Chandra Bose, the eminent Indian scientist, established that vegetation also contained this power. Through experiments he proved that if a vine was planted near a sapling, its growth was considerably accelerated in comparison with the vine not supported by the company of saplings.

While studying this energy, Dr. Charcot felt that the energy would soon gain in volume if it was given a suggestion to that effect. For instance, a person, argued Dr. Charcot, walks briskly if he is going to meet a likeable friend. It was a case of reciprocity of emotional make-up. The person, surely, does not walk that fast if he is going to see his enemy. Again, his face glows with radiance if he is told that he would see his beloved. What it implies is that he had in his organism the same quantum of magnetic power, which, however, fluctuated depending on the emotion he felt at a certain moment. In other words, emotion plays a significant role in controlling the magnetic power inherent in the individual.

One can see the role of feelings or emotions from an interesting development reported to have taken place in a cinema house. Once a physician and his wife both seated together were seeing a movie. After some time, the wife felt an oppressive headache and lost all interest in the movie. She could not bear the pain any more and began to insist on leaving for home.

The physician did not want to forego the pleasure of seeing the movie. He said to his wife: Nothing to feel worried about. This evening an agent gave me a sample pill of a perfect remedy for headache. I have the sample in my pocket and it will cure you of your headache.

As he said so, he took out one of the buttons of his trouser in the dark hall of the theatre and gave it to his wife. He asked her to put it into her mouth and continue to suck it.

In a few minutes the wife felt a big relief. Her headache was gone. She saw the movie pretty happily.

The headache was cured not because of any medicine. In fact, the wife had an implicit faith in her husband and in his capabilities. It was the implicit faith rather than any medicine which cured her of headache.

We come across a number of similar developments in life. While playing soccer, a certain player hurts his toe. The toe snaps into two and the blood gushes out. And yet being lost in the high emotion of a well-contested match, he hardly feels any pain in his toe. The moment the game is over and he looks at his injured toe, he screams out of pain. He wonders how he has been playing for an hour, despite the severe injury in his toe.

To take another instance, a person on his death-bed might long to eat a favourite delicacy before death. The delicacy, warn the physicians, might hasten his death. And yet, this being his last wish, they give him his favourite delicacy. The patient knows that it might be fatal. Nonetheless his eyes reveal a glow. No more does he bother about the ill-effects or otherwise of this or that delicacy. It is evident that his emotions got centred around that favourite delicacy.

To take yet another instance, suppose you accost a healthy and fast friend of yours by saying: What is the matter? You look so sad and pale today! Perhaps he may not believe you. Suppose a few more friends accost him with the same remark. In all certainty he will feel sick. When his so-called illness was repeatedly dinned into his ears by so many friends, he found no other way than to keep himself confined to bed. This was in spite of the fact that he was not ill. For you had impinged on him the idea that he was ill, which alone accounts for the fact that he fell ill.

To sum up: Magnetic power which the Indian *yogis* called *pran shakti* is inherent in every individual. Following certain spiritual practices, this energy can be developed. Once developed to a degree the energy will do miracles. Emotion or sentiment plays a crucial role in its development or non-development. It is emotion which gives a sharp edge or bluntness to this energy.

OO

3. IMPORTANT PRINCIPLES
OF HYPNOTISM

In the preceding chapter, an attempt has been made to describe both magnetic power and emotion. It is now explicit that every living being has in him magnetic power. By taking resort to certain spiritual practices we can further develop the magnetic power. We can have a greater concentration of this power in our physique. We can also transfer it to other organisms.

One gets a sense of achievement from this power if one strengthens it with emotion. For the energy generated through a blending of magnetic power and emotion is found to be extraordinarily powerful. It has the potential to unravel many mysteries which otherwise remain unknown.

Hypnotism, like any other science, is based on certain concrete principles. No doubt it has remained shrouded in the thick layers of secrecy for many years, which also explains why it remained stagnant. But the little we know of it has proved to be highly valuable in that it contributed a lot to improving the quality of life.

Outstanding Western and Eastern masters of hypnotism have formulated the following concrete and significant principles in this field. One must closely follow these principles if one wants to emerge as a successful hypnotist:

1. Any sane person, whether man or woman, can be a successful hypnotist. It recognises no distinction. It is not at all essential that one must be a genius to be a hypnotist. Again, it is entirely misleading to hold that this knowledge is divine or a God-gift. It is a science which one must learn steadily.

2. An insane or idiotic or mentally retarded person cannot be

hypnotised. The subject[1] or, in other words, the person to be hypnotised, needs be a person of normal intelligence. He should be able to distinguish between good and bad and know well that he is a 'subject' and is gong to be hypnotised for a particular purpose.

3. It is easier to hypnotise a 'subject' whose age is identical to that of the hypnotist. If the 'subject' is pretty older or far younger, the hypnotist may have either too much respect or condescension as the case may be, and not, in any case, total identity as the situation demands.

To take an example, the hypnotist, aged 30, may have his 'subject' between 20 and 40 years old. Otherwise, it is feared that confronted with a 'subject' either younger or older than his age group, the hypnotist may not easily identify himself with such differential age-groups.

According to the Western school, the more determined the 'subject' is, the easier he lends himself for the process of hypnotisation. The Indian school, however, holds a different view. Age, it argues, is in no way restrictive—any person of any age can be hypnotised.

The Indian school further holds that a single hypnotist can mass-hypnotise hundreds of men and women at one go. It did not, for instance, take more than a moment for the ancient Indian sage Vishwamitra to hypnotise the 60,000 sons of King Sagar and work up deathly inactivity in each one of them.

4. A 'subject' must not be made to act or behave in a way repugnant to the tenets of his religion or personal taste. A *Brahmin*, for example, cannot be made to eat non-vegetarian food during his hypnotic sleep. For, it should be noted, the 'subject' while undergoing hypnotisation, has his outer mind reduced to sleepiness, but not the inner mind, which sharply reacts to anything repugnant to the tenets of his religion or personal taste. If persisted, it might break off the trance.

5. The belief of some persons that hypnotic sleep might end

1. *Subject*: Also called 'medium'.

up in a prolonged or endless sleep without foundation. The moment the trance is withdrawn, the sleepiness of the 'subject' vanishes and he is restored to his consciousness.

At times, hypnotic sleep is overtaken by natural sleep. In that case, the 'subject' sleeps a little longer and feels infinitely healthier after he wakes up.

Over ages not a single report has been received when the 'subject' was not restored to consciousness following hypnotic sleep.

6. In the state of hypnotic sleep, the inner potential of the 'subject' lends itself for a better realisation, further development and right orientation. Precisely, for this reason, he comes to see things far into the future or deep into the past. Suppose, owing to a severe head injury, he forgot his own name and everything about himself and his family. Now, in the state of hypnotic trance, he is likely to recall what he had forgotten clean.

Hypnotic sleep helps in such cases. While asleep hypnotically he easily recalls the moments of the past such as his own name, his family and the principal events of his family.

7. Hypnotic experiments have proved particularly useful for release from bad habits. During hypnotic sleep the 'subject' could be suggested that such and such bad habit of his is eating into his health. It is likely to help him give up the chronic bad habit. The inner mind of the 'subject' receives and accepts the suggestions during hypnotic sleep. He does not forget the suggestions made during hypnotic sleep after he is dehypnotised. He acts upon these suggestions and gets rid of bad habits.

8. While asleep hypnotically, one's organs of perception and action, each one of them, remain quite active, although they appear to be dormant. In fact, one's talent and intelligence get sharpened. He smells and hears better.

9. Hypnotism makes the outer mind asleep by contriving an artificial sleep. Nonetheless the inner mind remains awake

and lends itself to the control of the hypnotist. In this state, the inner mind accepts and acts upon in whatever manner the hypnotist calls upon it to do.

10. Every care should be taken to ensure that the hypnotist is well-equipped and competent beyond doubt before he begins to experiment on his 'subjects'. A half-baked knowledge leads to immense harm.

11. It will be risky to presume that one can take resort to hypnotism for mere fun. For the outer mind being put to hypnotic sleep repeatedly might give rise to certain intractable complications beyond any treatment or solution. So, induction of hypnosis for the sake of fun is strictly prohibited.

Nevertheless we have come across any right thinking people being assailed by a measure of scepticism on the true nature of hypnotism. The several questions they raise can be categorised in the form of the following questions. We have provided answers so that our readers are left in no doubt.

Question: What is Hypnotism?

Answer: Hypnotism is a science through which the outer mind of an individual can be brought to sleep and the inner mind roused and governed so as to obtain desired results. Thus, we see the human being has two minds. The outer mind remains conscious while the inner mind is always active. At times, we have noticed that the hand which slips to go near the fire, withdraws itself suddenly. The outer mind being lost in some other contemplation has not noticed the hand reaching near the fire, while the inner mind being always active, gets it withdrawn from the impending danger. The point is that the inner mind remains as active as the outer mind.

According to Dr. Burnham, a Western hypnotist, hypnotism is based on three postulates:

1. Hope: It offers itself as the most important and active base to reach the state of the hypnotised.

2. Will: It accelerates the state of hypnotisation and further develops it to achieve integrity.

3. Effect: It is through effect that the hypnotist succeeds in establishing a more effective influence on his 'subject'.

The word 'hope' merits a short note. By hope we mean that the 'medium' must have implicit faith in the capabilities of the hypnotist. To create in him an impression like this, it is essential that the hypnotist conducts himself very seriously. The hypnotist at the same time must project himself in such a manner so that he (the subject) comes to believe that he (hypnotist) is an outstanding expert in his field.

As the hypnotist advances in his work, he will gradually come to know how he should conduct himself, what all he must do and with what instruments he must equip himself. Everything about the hypnotist—his manner of talking, his conduct, his style of work, his method, his demeanour and apparel and above all, his personality, will have the potential to rouse the desired hypnotic effect.

By the following three stages, we obtain hypnotisation:

A. Ordinary: While in this stage the 'medium' finds it beyond himself to open his eyes. Gradually his hands and legs go out of his control. He does not know what he is doing and what his state of being is.

B. Medium: This stage puts the 'medium' to a deeper hypnotic sleep. While his capacity to receive suggestions remains very limited, his inner mind is receptive to all orders placed on it.

C. Unconscious: This stage marks the deepest hypnotic sleep the 'medium' graduates to. He receives in a proper way whatever suggestions or biddings he is called upon to follow. He acts up to it in a proper way. It is actually an artificial sleep, and as he wakes up to his consciousness, he recalls whatever he was told in the hypnotic sleep.

This is the ultimate stage, a rounded one. In this stage, the 'medium' loses all control over himself and he simply follows whatever he is told to do. He feels himself totally at the disposal of the hypnotist.

If the 'medium' is suggested at this stage that he would have no pain at all even if his body is sliced into pieces, he would actually not feel any pain after the hypnotist literally cuts a limb off his body. In the U.S. surgical operations are conducted following this method. In Europe, too, risky operations are performed after obtaining a similar stage.

If the 'medium' is suggested at this stage in chilly winter season that the day is burning hot and the heat today has become unbearable, he would put off his clothes and would feel the blazing heat of the summer.

Working on this suggestion, the Indian *yogis* used to perch themselves high above the snowy summits of the Himalayas, a mountain range of snow and ice. Where normally nobody, with all his protective clothes, could think of spending a minute, the *yogis* in scanty clothes used to roam happily.

Question: Can one hypnotise oneself?

Answer: The hypnotist can hypnotise others and make him do things as he wants. Following the other method, he can hypnotise himself, which is called self-hypnotisation.

In ancient times, the *yogis* used to sit in *samadhi*[1] for long durations. Even today there are many *yogis* who take recourse to *samadhi* for 10 to 15 days. It is self-hypnotisation which accounts for this capacity. In a situation like this, the hypnotist suggests to his own outer mind to fall asleep. He obtains *samadhi* through self-hypnotisation. Nevertheless his inner mind remains fully active, with the result that all his limbs keep functioning as usual and he remains alive.

Question: Is it true that only the volitionless person can be hypnotised?

Answer: No. It is the other way round. It is easier to hypnotise a person of strong determination than a volitionless person. The point is that one proves to be a better 'medium' only when one follows the suggestions of the hypnotist. Normally one finds a person of a better understanding and stronger determination responding to the suggestions in a better manner.

Indeed hypnotism has been a proven instrument to make one's volition stronger. It ensures a better memory too.

1. *Samadhi:* A self-absorbed spiritual meditation during which the meditator loses his or her entity and becomes one with the Supreme Being.

Question: Do you think a majority of people can be hypnotised?

Answer: Every person is emotional and he must necessarily give vent to his emotional urges. This being the state of a majority of people, one can hypnotise them as normally as one does an individual. But the person, who is ruthless and devoid of mercy and emotion, cannot be hypnotised. The person, who goes by facts and who believes in only what he sees, will be unresponsive to suggestions and so he cannot be hypnotised.

Question: Does hypnotism lessen and eliminate pain?

Answer: Now it is common place that surgical operations in Western countries are performed after hypnotising the patients. The patients, once hypnotised, do not feel any pain at all. Besides, hypnotised patients respond to, and act upon, the suggestions. In the U.S. women have painless delivery through this medium.

Question: Can one give up bad habits like smoking and drinking through hypnotism?

Answer: Yes, one can, if the 'medium' under hypnotic sleep is told of the evil effects of these bad habits and if he is given a suggestion that he is capable of giving up these ingrained bad habits. He will remember these suggestions even after regaining consciousness and he will start hating these bad habits.

Similarly he can sort out any complex he may have in his make-up.

Question: Can we hypnotise somebody against his own wish?

Answer: No. Unless one offers co-operation, one cannot be hypnotised. Besides, he must have implicit faith in the hypnotist.

Question: Who lends oneself to be a better 'medium'?

Answer: He must be an understanding type of person. He must follow the language we speak. He must concentrate his attention on whatever we say. It is only such a person who can be a good 'medium'.

Question: Is it difficult to wake up the hypnotised man?

Answer: No. Hypnotisation brings about an artificial sleep and when this sleep is terminated, the hypnotised person wakes up.

Even before he is hypnotised, he is told he must wake up once the hypnotist claps thrice. Cracking fingers or simply repeating 'Wake up' are the other signs which the hypnotist similarly uses.

If no attempt is made to bring the 'medium' back to consciousness, we should not unduly worry about it because the artificial sleep after some time changes into natural sleep. When the natural sleep would have run its full course, he will wake up as normally as people do. In the process, the hypnotised person does not feel subjected to any pain or suffering. On the other hand, he feels strengthened by a new spirit and enthusiasm.

It is, therefore, wrong to suggest that the hypnotised man does not wake up after hypnotic sleep. To hypnotise the person initially is quite difficult, but once this stage is gone through, the rest will take care of itself.

Question: Does the 'medium', after he wakes up from hypnotic sleep, remember what all he was suggested in course of his hypnotic sleep?

Answer: The hypnotist suggests everything to the inner mind. The inner mind as we know perfectly remains active always. So, once the hypnotist tells the hypnotised man that he will remember whatever he is being told now, he will in all certainty remember every word of the suggestions.

When the hypnotised person recalls during his hypnotic sleep past events or incidents of his childhood, he will remember even these details after he wakes up.

However, should the 'medium' be suggested during the hypnotic sleep that he will or should not remember the things he is being told, it is likely that he will forget all these things after he wakes up. Even if he is told that he has forgotten these things, he will lend no credence to it.

Question: Can hypnotism enrich memory?

Answer: Viewed objectively, it alone will go down as a great achievement of hypnotism. For he remembers during hypnotic sleep what all took place in his life. Besides, such ganglions of his brain as were lying dormant or inactive over a long time get activated and develop in the process. When ganglions of this sort are activated, his memory gets strengthened and he develops the capacity to remember things.

Often some persons lose their memory. In such cases, hypnotism is the only medium which can restore memory.

Question: Is it a fact that only highly intelligent and highly educated persons can be hypnotists?

Answer: No, it is not so. Any person following right practice can be a hypnotist. He must have a strong will-power. He must at the same time, know the art of conversation. If he has a resonant voice and also a taste for the right apparel, he can be even a better hypnotist. One who can inspire confidence in others will emerge as a successful hypnotist.

Question: Can a hypnotised person be made to commit crimes?

Answer: The answer is a qualified 'yes'. We have already shown that there are three stages in hypnosis. In the ordinary and medium stages, one cannot make the hypnotised person commit any crimes. But when he reaches the third stage, he grows into a perfect slave of the hypnotist. He thinks it is his duty to be at the behest of the hypnotist.

In a situation like this, particularly when the hypnotist has already given him a set of orders during the hypnotic sleep, he will not only remember the orders, but will feel restless until the orders are carried out. It is this which gives him mental peace.

Contemporary European press is replete with such news items. It has grown into a big problem for the governments over there. It is a big problem for the judiciary in Europe to fix responsibility for such crimes as one commits not on his own, but at the bidding of others.

It is only in the third stage that one can be suggested to commit crimes, which is not possible in the earlier stages.

Question: Is it proper to make use of hypnotism in the field of surgery?

Answer: Modern surgery is indebted to hypnotism. Without taking resort to chloroform the surgeons perform operations largely with the help of hypnotism. Administering chloroform was not without certain complications. A heavier dose would prove fatal while a lighter dose would wake up the patient prematurely.

It is only through hypnotism that the problem could be solved. In Europe and the U.S., use of chloroform has been more or less given up. In the field of heart surgery, the surgeons make use of only hypnotism. It has given them cent per cent good results.

Question: Can one hypnotise oneself?

Answer: As a matter of fact, hypnotism works on the principle of self-hypnotism. Dr. Burnham has already explained that one can hypnotise oneself without taking resort to the services of the hypnotist.

In hypnotism, it is essential that the 'medium' has implicit faith in the hypnotist. If he is capable of responding to the suggestions planted on him, he will easily lend himself to the process of hypnotisation, and thus derive all benefits therefrom.

As it has already been explained in the foregoing pages, the Western hypnotic science developed in a particular way, while its beginning suggests it was integral to the Indian practices. In the Indian philosophy, this practice is called *Pran Vidya*.

In other words, one is accepted as a hypnotist if he practises *Pranayama* and *Yoga*. By virtue of this practice, his inner power gets further strengthened. It brings off a spurt in his innate self-confidence, which makes him a successful hypnotist.

The Indian *yogis* practised self-hypnotism and remained in the state of hypnosis. It enabled them to gain control over their organs of perception and action. It was through such a vigorous self-control that they could accomplish impossible deeds which are considered miracles in the present age of science.

Even today, with the help of these practices, we can achieve a similar *siddhi*[1]. We shall gain complete control over body and strengthen magnetic power to become a successful hypnotist.

In his book, Dr. William Browne recommended the following general practice:

First step: Lie in a comfortable posture and allow the mind and the brain to relax.

Second step: Activate the inner mind by gaining control over it.

When the inner mind is activated, it generates a special kind of magnetic power, and will result in a developed concentration of mind, memory and self-confidence. It is this power which makes an individual a competent and successful hypnotist.

OO

1. *Siddhi:* Divine grace or spiritual salvation attainable through austere religious practice.

4. PRINCIPLES OF HYPNOTISM: THE INDIAN APPROACH

In India, hypnotism, an ancient science, was rooted in the *Yoga* system; and called variously at times as art of hypnotism or as knowledge of hypnotism, the science has been part and parcel of the Indian spiritualism.

Indian philosophy and Indian spiritualism have always been integral to the *Yoga* system. *Yoga* means union. In spiritual terms it means the union of the soul and the *Brahma*[1]. The concept of union as logically extended has come to mean the union of the devotee and God, man and the Almighty, the individual and the universal and the body and the creation. Substantially, the ultimate object of the *Yogic* practices has been to achieve a profound concentration of one's inner self in total submission to the Almighty. It is only by way of total submission to the Almighty that one finds oneself granted divine grace. This benediction is called *Yoga* or hypnotism, in other words.

In the Indian philosophy the concept of *Yoga* has come to mean a severe control of, and total negation of the desires and inclinations of the *Chitta*[2]. Once we obtain this, we achieve a total identity with the Almighty. In this state, the individual is not confronted with any barriers when he wants to see beyond—into the past and the future. Such a person can activate the entire universe at his bidding.

Indeed hypnotic power can be achieved through the medium of the *Yoga* too. Broadly, the Yoga has five kinds: *Hath Yoga, Dhyana Yoga, Karma Yoga, Bhakti Yoga* and *Jnana Yoga*. This categorisation was made possible because, basically, man has

---

1. *Brahma:* The Absolute Being.
2. *Chitta:* The faculty of the mind or the mental awakening.

five important powers. For instance, *Hath Yoga* derives from *Pran Shakti*, *Dhyana Yoga* from mental power, *Karma Yoga* from activity, *Bhakti Yoga* from emotion and *Jnana Yoga* from highly developed intellect. Only after establishing relations of this kind does man transcend his individual and submerge in the universal. According to the *Puranas*[1] Lord Siva is the founder of the *yogic* knowledge and for this reason, He is called *Yogiraj*—the king of *Yogis*. The *yoga* knowledge initiated by Lord Siva was carried on by subsequent saints and seers. Of the treatises available in the modern times, the more important are *Hath Yoga Pradeepika*, *Yoga Darshan*, *Gaurava Samhita*, *Hath Yoga Sar* and *Kundak Yoga*. *Patanjali's Yoga Darshan* is said to be authentic in this field.

According to *Patanjali*, there are eight stages of the *Yoga*: *Yama*, *Niyama*, *Asana*, *Pranayama*, *Pratyahara*, *Dharana*, *Dhyana* and *Samadhi*. The first five are external and the rest three are internal.

1. **Yama:** An unfailing adherence to the tenets of non-violence, truth, integrity, abstinence from sexual and secular pleasures, and non-possessiveness is called *Yama*.

2. **Niyama:** A devotion to health, contentment, austerity, purity and spiritual meditation is called *Niyama*.

3. **Asana:** Sitting in a comfortable posture absorbedly attentive and intent is called *Asana*.

4. **Pranayama:** Preservation of vital energy in the body through exhaling, inhaling and controlling the movements of breath is called *Pranayama*.

5. **Pratyahara:** To deflect the senses from their physical objects and harmonise them with the faculty of the mind is said to be *Pratyahara*.

6. **Dharana:** To organise total concentration of one's mind in a particular thought is said to be *Dharana*.

7. **Dhyana:** Concentration of the mind on a given object undisturbed by the presence of other objects is called *Dhyana*.

8. **Samadhi:** Total absorption in the target object oblivious of

---

1. *Puranas:* The Hindu mythology.

one's own existence is called *Samadhi*.

When the first five stages are achieved and the *Sadhak* achieves perfection in all these stages, he is presumed to have qualified for the remaining three stages. The *Sadhak* is advised to accomplish the first five stages before he enters the realm of the remaining three.

The *yogi* achieves absolute identity with the five elements—earth, water, fire, air and ether. He also attains a perfect harmony with the objects of these elements—from, *rasa*[1], smell, word and touch.

It is only when he accomplishes the tasks of identity and harmony as described above does the *yogi* attain the eight *siddhis*. The eight *siddhis* are:

1.	Anima	5.	Prapti
2.	Mahima	6.	Prakamya
3.	Laghima	7.	Vashitwa
4.	Garima	8.	Eeshatwa

The *yogi* who succeeds in attaining all these eight *siddhis* will not be wanting in anything in his life. A mere wish will get him whatever he wants. Every word he utters proves to be nothing but truth. He is crowned with the title of *Yogiraj*—king of *Yogis*.

Among the *Hath Yoga* practices the first is awakening the *Kundalini*[2], In the body between the genital organ and the anus is found a dormant power which is called *sushumna*[3]. On the two sides of the *Sushumna* are found two nerves—*Ida* and *Pingala*. These are located close to the umbilical region. These three together are called *trinetra*. One who can make his *sushumna* travel upward through the spinal column via the point in front of the coccyx (the point where it enters the spinal column) and make it terminate at the centre of *sahasrara*[1] is said to have awakened his *kundalini* (consciousness or awareness). The *kundalini* which assumes the forms of any one

---

1. *Rasa:* Commonly it means savour or flavour. In the present context inner or true significance.
2 *Kundalini:* Roused consciousness of the vital force latent in a creature.
3. *Sushumna:* A psychic passage visible as the shaft of light.

of the objects such as serpent or nectar or arrow or trident is visualised to move through these nerves. He is blessed with divine knowledge and omniscience. He changes into Lord Siva Himself. The terms 'impossible' and 'difficult' lose meaning to Him.

Hypnotism is a part of this *Yoga* power. It is through this power that one can develop one's mental power as well as will-power. These developed powers ensure mastery of hypnotism. Primarily the following benefits accrue from these practices:

1. The body grows into a healthy and well-chiselled organism.
2. It helps develop mental power.
3. It ensures an all-pervasive peace.
4. It helps develop spiritual power.

YOGA NIDRA

Artificial sleep or hypnotism which we work up by way of influencing others or extending influence on self through spiritual power in either case is called Yoga Nidra in the Indian philosophy.

It helps memory. It helps us rise to great heights, and live a balanced life.

The yoga nidra is calculated to achieve the following:

1. It can put the 'subject' to artificial sleep.
2. The 'subject' while asleep hypnotically can be made to follow the suggestions of the sadhak-the hypnotist.
3. It helps enrich his imagination. It is due to this highly developed imagination that he is in a position to answer all questions.
4. Through yoga nidra the sadhak can make the 'subject' follow his injunctions.

The sadhak, besides, can hypnotise himself and be benefited as much as he could benefit the 'subject'. Viewed from any angle

---

1. *Sahasrara:* The highest psychic centre or *Chakra* wherein the *yogi* attains union of his individual self and God.

it does good rather than harm.

One must always remember that the yoga nidra or artificial sleep is distinct from natural sleep. In case of natural sleep one sleeps completely, which does not give him any scope to respond to the suggestions of the hypnotist. However, in case of hypnotic sleep, it is only the outer mind of the individual which is put to sleep while his inner mind remains fully awake and responds to all suggestions of the hypnotist.

Viewed from a certain angle the artificial sleep is hardly different from drowsiness or light sleep. In this situation the 'subject' makes full submission to the hypnotist.

The foundation of the *yoga nidra* is spiritual power. In fact it is found in every individual to some degree. If he so chooses the individual can develop it by a set of special practices and exercises. *Karma Shakti*[1], *Jnana Shakti*[2], *Ichchha Shakti*[3] and others are some of the forms of this spiritual power. It is only by rousing and developing these powers that the *sadhak* can achieve a completeness.

Elsewhere we have referred to *Pran Shakti*. In reality the principal base of the hypnotist is this *Pran Shakti*. It is only when he develops this *shakti* the hypnotist succeeds in his attempts. In him it gives rise to a particular kind of *pran* consciousness, and also to a developed form of magnetic power. Accordingly a particular kind of glow and attraction characterises his eyes. His fingers, magnetically enriched, develop power to hypnotise anybody by a mere touch.

The *yoga nidra* puts to sleep the outer mind. The inner mind remains very active. He loses his intellectual consciousness.

PRAN SHAKTI

According to the Indian philosophy the *pran shakti* is universal. Every animate being receives it through breathing. Actually it

---

1. *Karma Shakti:* The power of activity or work.
2. *Jnana Shakti:* The power of knowledge.
3. *Ichchha Shakti:* The will-power.

is formed from air, sunlight, earth, ether and others. The individual is attracted to this force. It is on the circulation of this energy that the individual health remains balanced and organised.

According to the Indian *yoga* studies there are eight centres or *chakras* in the human physique. The energy which is identified as *kundalini* flows through the psychic passages, known as *nadi*. It is this nadi which connects all these centres. These *chakras* are: *Mooladhar, Swadhisthan, Surya, Anhad, Vishudha, Agni, Sahasrar* and *Brahmarandhra*.

It is *pran shakti* which influences and governs these eight centres.

As already explained, earlier man imbibes energy every moment in his life to keep himself active. One expends and yet needs it. So if it is stored at one place and given out to others by way of suggestions, one can have one's desired wishes fulfilled in all certainty. The energy having been concentrated at one place and used to give it out to others is called will-power. The process is like receiving sunrays into a convex lens and exposing a piece of paper to the total volume of the solar heat.

Ancient Indian literature is replete with such instances. The great sage Agastya, to take an instance, had drunk the entire sea at one go. Durwasa, to take another instance, had burnt the 60,000 sons of King Sagar at one time. These instances are not figments of imagination. It was also due to the high concentration of the *pran shakti* which these meditators used to store in their body.

Will-power can be controlled in the same manner as the *pran shakti* is controlled.

In order to gain control over the pran shakti it is essential that we achieve pranayama. For it is this which ensures in the mind a total concentration of thoughts. It is by virtue of this concentration are the past and the future revealed.

Although it is not possible to achieve this sort of concentration in the noise-polluted world today, one can nevertheless practise pranayama at a lonely place, say, the riverbank or the secluded mountain cave.

PRANAYAMA

As already explained, *pranayama* achieves a total control over thoughts. It is not merely controlling one's breathing—the inhaling and the exhaling. It is on the other hand a discipline which helps one establish a total control over one's *pran shakti*.

In his volume *Raj Yoga* Swami Vivekananda explained that the cosmos is made of two elements called *prana* and ether. The creation was made possible through a harmonious blending of these two elements.

All tangible objects are born of the ether. It was through it that the sun and the moon assumed their forms. The human physique came into existence through the ether. All moving and active objects of the world owe their existence to the ether.

Although the ether is very minute and difficult for anybody to see, the *yogi* or *sadhak* who succeeds in gaining control over the *pran shakti* will certainly be able to see it.

It was only from the ether that the creation was made possible. Whatever one comes to see when the earth is overtaken by the deluge recedes to the ether. Man gets his form and *pran* that is life from the ether. The ether is all pervasive, so is the *pran shakti*.

Creation is made possible because man is endowed with *pran shakti*. When the *pran shakti* recedes into the sky, man too does so. Thus the ether and the *pran shakti* are interrelated. The ether is created out of *pran* and the ether assumes completion with the decay or death of the *pran*. It is through ether that man derives his *pran shakti* which, again, ensures his strength, thinking, life, etc.

So much so the Indian philosophy has made it very explicit that each and every human action is controlled by *pran shakti*, and because it is integral to the ether, so only absorption of the *pran shakti* in the ether is *pranayama*.

It is not at all necessary the hypnotist should be well versed in all the actions of the *pranayama*. However, he is expected to know all about its practical aspects if he wants to know the subtleties of hypnotism. A fresh and unpolluted air as also a solitary place is essential for *pranayama*. If practised with deep mental concentration, the *pranayama* will certainly develop our spiritual power, with the result we achieve a completion in all *sadhanas* and may be accepted as a complete man or *yogiraj*.

The *sadhak* must know the following actions for normal *pranayama*.

PRANAYAMA—ACTION 1

Lie on your back on a plain surface. Stretch your legs straight and keep your hands parallel to your body. Close your eyes. Keep lying and do not move any part of the body.

Ensure that no part of your body gets activated. See that no thought whatsoever disturbs your mind. Allow the body loose so that each limb relaxes to the fullest extent.

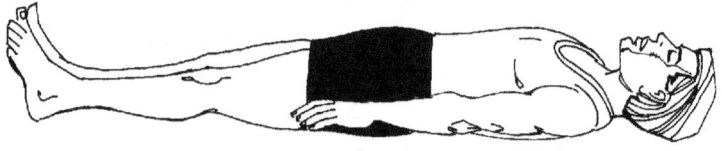

Pranayama—Action 1

Gradually ensure that all your limbs, from head to foot, feel totally relaxed. First you make your head idea-free. Then the eyes, the neck, the hands and the toes and other fingers and even the mind be made relaxed and idea-free. Harbour no ideas, no thoughts, no feelings in your brain.

In the beginning you will find it very difficult to free your brain from ideas. However, practise regularly. After some time you will be able to make your brain free from ideas and thoughts. You will be able to gain full control over your brain.

Nonetheless you will find that the brain is yet being assailed by some stray thought. It forces itself slowly. Initially you will be thought-free only for a minute. However as you continue to prolong your exercise the duration of the state of being thought-free will also increase. Now at this stage you continue to practise and obtain this state for fifteen minutes. Slowly and steadily you bring the duration down to, say, a minute.

When the mind has been made totally free from all ideas and your body being actionless is reduced to a real passivity, this state called *Shava*[1] *Sadhana* resembles death in life. At the same time a special kind of energy passes all over your body.

PRANAYAMA—ACTION 2

This practice should be resorted to only after one has gone through the earlier practice.

Lie on your back and stretch your legs and hands free and reduce your mind to total freedom from thoughts. Seal your lips. Inhale deeply through both the nostrils. Now round your lips and give out the air breathed in slowly. When you do so you will hear a whistling sound being made.

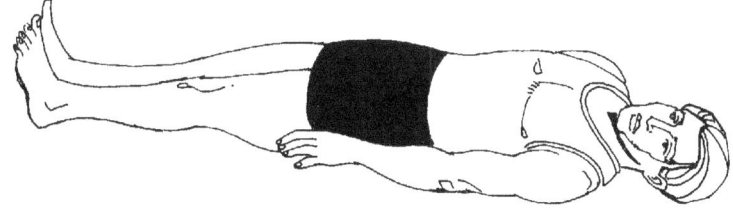

Pranayama—Action 2

It must be ensured that one must inhale through one nostril only. At that time the mouth should remain closed. When one seeks to exhale the breath the nose should be blocked and the entire breath should be given out through the mouth.

In the beginning one must practise this exercise for 2 to 3 minutes. Steadily one must prolong the practice. Now one can practise the exercise up to 15 minutes. The implication is that one must inhale deeply to fill his lungs, allow the air to remain in the lungs for 3 to 4 minutes and then gradually release it out.

One must take note of the fact that the foundation of the *pranayama* is one's capacity to retain the breath inside. Gradually, over a long and sustained practice, the *sadhak* should increase the duration of retention. In no case should he be impatient, for any hurry on that score is fraught with grave danger.

Shava: Dead body.

PRANAYAMA—ACTION 3

First the *sadhak* should successfully practise the first and second actions. He must have accomplished the reality of an idea-free mind. He must also have developed the extraordinary capacity to retain breath for some time. When he is holding his breath, he should wish that the *pran shakti* he has retained within is circulated in his head, shoulders, eyes, neck, heart, navel and legs. In every limb and in every pore of his physique the *pran shakti*, he must feel, has made itself present.

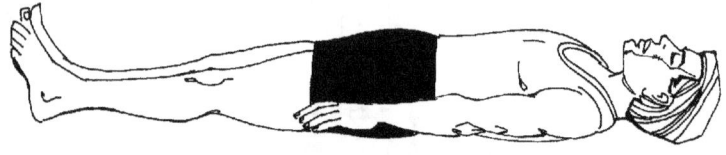

Pranayama—Action 3

Now being confident that the *pran shakti* is already in circulation in a given limb, he should seek to extend it to the other limb.

Initially as the breathing was restrained, one would be able to suggest the circulation of the *pran shakti* only in a couple of limbs. Late as the practice sustains one will be able to have it circulated in more limbs. So the *sadhak* must increase his practice and he must develop it to the point that the *pran shakti* overtakes the entire physique at one go.

The *sadhak* himself will feel that the limb which witnesses a high circulation of *pran shakti* experiences a sort of sensation, which is the sign of the limb having come under the total impact of this *shakti*.

In reality the sensation is nothing but the circulation of the *pran shakti* at a good speed.

SHAKTI CHAKRA

It is only when one finds the body is saturated with the *pran shakti* derived from *pranayama* that one should advance to the practice of *shakti chakra*. It may be noted that the *shakti chakra* produces magnetic power in the eyes of the *sadhak*. Besides it helps build his concentration.

Shakti Chakra—American Method

Select a secluded, airy, ventilated and well-lighted room. Draw a sketch of *shakti chakra*. In the U.S. they draw this *chakra* in a different way. In Greece in a yet different way. However, the power it exudes is roughly the same.

Draw the *shakti chakra* in bold black ink on a white thick paper. Fix it on the wall at your eye level. Now be seated on a thick cushion at least two feet away facing the sketch. Fix your eyes on the sketch. You must ensure that you resort to this exercise only when you are feeling healthy, not exhausted or worried and you must be feeling quite cheerful.

As you are seated on the cushion, stretch your hands and legs free and relaxed. Work up a feeling as though you are feeling very light riding on the waves of the ocean. Please ensure that no thoughts whatsoever assail your mind. Fix your eyes and have a steadfast gaze at the sketch.

The *sadhak* must continue to practise like this without batting an eye-lid. The more you gaze at the sketch the better. The duration of the practice must be prolonged gradually. When the eyes begin to go watery better you suspend the practice. You must resume it the next day. As you continue to go ahead with your practice, you must work up a feeling in your psyche that your eyes are gaining in power, and that your mind is emerging thought-free.

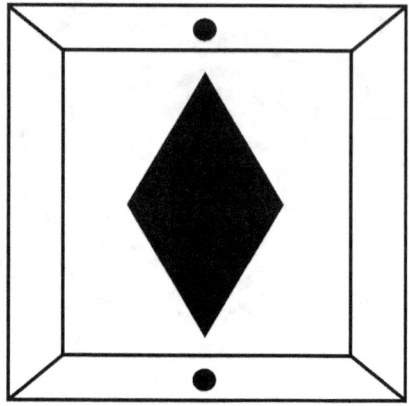

Shakti Chakra—Greek Method

After a protracted practice over some days the *sadhak* will feel a particular type of power emerging in his eyes. With the help of this power he can hypnotise anybody in a matter of a few minutes.

After a few days of regular practice, the *Chakra* will seem to be moving away from its location. It will seem to be moving up or down or right or left. As you see the *Chakra* moving away from its location the *sadhak* must give it a fixed gaze and give it such a look that it comes back to its fixed location.

After some time the *sadhak* will see in the *Chakra* some beautiful or horrible pictures or scenes. It indicates that you have achieved the requisite concentration and that you are going about the job in right earnest.

As you continue to practise you might see two or three *Chakras* in place of one *Chakra*. It is also a sign of your success.

You might also see in the *Chakra* mountains, rivers, tanks and deserts. Might be they are familiar to you. Might be they are unfamiliar. The unfamiliar ones already exist on the earth. Possibly you have not come across them. You might, to your utter astonishment, see them one day.

The scenes which you see in the *Chakra* were part of your past or part of your future which you might see at a future point.

Such sights indicate that your power of concentration is increasing. You should now gain control over what you see in the *Chakra*. It means that you should try to see only the sights of your choice. You may, for instance, wish to see who is sitting in your bedroom situated at a place far off or what your wife or mother is doing at home at that moment. After a regular practice of the *Chakra* it should be possible for you to see the desired sight on the *Chakra*. Perhaps you may also hear their actual voices.

A regular practice of *Chakra* will equip your eyes with hypnotic eyes. A mere steadfast look at any other person would bring him down totally submitted to you. He will do whatever you ask him to do provided it does not conflict with his basic philosophy.

To test as to what extent you have succeeded in your practice, better you take the following exercises too:

1. As you are walking, fix your eye on the neck of the person walking ahead of you. Now work up a wish that the person should look back at you.

2. You will be surprised to see that the man looks back at you as you wished. Suppose you are attending a conference or a party. A person—man or woman—is seated there with his or her neck opposite. Now you fix your gaze at his or her neck and work up a feeling that he or she should look at you. You will be pleasantly surprised to see that the person does exactly in the manner you wished.

3. Ask a person to wrap his palm with a handkerchief or hide it (the palm) in his pocket or beneath the table. Now fix your gaze at any other portion of his hand and start thinking that his palm is getting hot. Tell your friend that his palm has already got hot. You will be surprised to know that your friend will also feel his palm very hot.

4. Ask your friend to lay the reverse of his palm on the table. Gaze at the palm and suggest that the hand is rising all by itself. Tell him that his hand is rising although he himself has not wanted it. He will feel surprised to see that his hand is rising and floating although he has not wanted it.

One must continue to do all these exercises. One should not

feel put off if he does not succeed in the beginning. One will certainly succeed if one continues to practise for some time.

LIGHT ON CHAKRA

After a regular practice over a length of time the *sadhak* will have a refreshingly new experience. He will begin to see around the *shakti chakra* a thin ray of golden light. Gradually the golden light will have a wider spread-out and the whole of the *shakti chakra* will seem to reflect this light.

One must continue with this practice. At a certain stage one will see the golden light changing into a blue light. After some time the blue light will turn into a green light. Soon the green light will change into sunlight. So much so the *shakti chakra* will start shining with the brilliance of the sun.

In real terms the *Chakra* remains as it is. It does not change into the sun. It is actually your eyes which shine with the brilliance of the sun. It is this glare which gets reflected in the *shakti chakra*. It also interacts with your eyes. Meanwhile your eyes go so lustrous that wherever you cast a sight, it will light up like a torch. In a way this practice is calculated to generate a special glow in the eyes.

In order to preserve the glow in his eyes, the *sadhak* will have to observe the following regulations:

1. Avoid non-vegetarian food spices, hard drinks and acidity causing foods.
2. Exercise total control over your mind. Passions such as anger, vanity, hate must remain subdued.
3. Think twice before you begin to take up any job. It is essential so that you do not repeat for what you have done.
4. Do not involve yourself in such activities as are forbidden under religious and oral injunctions.
5. Do not indulge in silly jobs such as dangling your legs, cracking your fingers, cutting finger nails with teeth, etc.
6. Do not apologize unless warranted.
7. Maintain a spotlessly clear physique and a totally guiltless mentality. It will keep you fresh.

8. Do not feel concerned over trivial things. Nor should you break into intermittent laughter unnecessarily. You must keep your mind under your total control.

9. Do not see tawdry sights.

Practise *shakti chakra* regularly. Later, after some amount of practice, you better begin to imagine that a beautiful god is seated in the *chakra*. Now you work up a wish in your own mind that you should look as handsome, glorious and impressive as the god of the *chakra*. As you practise like it for some time, you will see a remarkable change within yourself.

HYPNOTIC POWER IN THE EYES

As already argued earlier, a regular practice of the *chakra* will get your eyes a special kind of magnetic power. Soon you will be highly popular and your friends' circle will widen more and more.

At times you could join a crowd. Fix your gaze on the necks of roughly 15 to 20 persons, and work up a wish that they look back at you. Soon as the wish is worked up, not only one, but all of them will look back at you.

Whenever you talk with any person, look deeply into his eyes. When you give a handshake, you better have a good feel of his hand and for this purpose, press his hand roundly. Do not allow him to press your hand. Your voice should be sonorous and sweet.

Act upon these simple pieces of advice and keep the hypnotic power of your eyes intact.

∞

5. TRATAK

Hatha Yoga Pradeepika, the authentic and celebrated treatise on *hatha yoga*, has called *tratak* a task among the six yogic tasks. To accomplish the supreme achievement in life as well as *yoga* it is indispensable that one keeps one's body wholly pure physically. The *pranayama* ensures a purification of this sort but it takes a long time. The treatise, therefore, recommends the following techniques for purification of the human body.

1. **Vasti:** Following this technique one inhales water through the anus up into the stomach, which cleanses the great intestines and other parts of the stomach.

2. **Dhauti:** Have a piece of fine cloth at least 15 feet long and one foot wide. Make it wet and pass it through the mouth It will clean the alimentary canal and remove the cough.

3. **Nauli:** The method of massaging and strengthening abdominal organs. One squats in a sitting posture called *padmasana* and then one performs a special kind of *pranayama* and by virtue of sheer will-power rotates his navel from left to right and vice-versa.

4. **Neti:** To draw water through one nostril and then release it through the nose and the mouth. It ensures cleansing of the nasal passage. Much in the same way one could have cleansing by inserting a cotton string through a nostril and bringing it out through the mouth. It ensures removal of all cough.

5. **Kapalaghati:** A series of *pranayama* techniques for purifying the front portion of the brain.

6. **Tratak:** A process of concentrating one's gaze at a point or a flame without batting an eye-lid. It enriches eye-sight and power of concentration.

Of the six techniques mentioned above, *tratak* is supreme, for it fixes one's gaze and ensures a thought-free mind. Once you close your eyes, you will have a quicker and surer concentration. In real terms *tratak* is a preliminary practice of hypnotism because it helps develop the hypnotic power of the eyes. It is with the aid of the hypnotic power of the eyes that one can hypnotise others. It is, therefore, indispensable for a practitioner of hypnotism. A regular practice of *tratak* will give us success in *dhyana-sadhana*[1]. It is only by virtue of this success one can get into the mind of the others and ascertain what all is going on in their minds. One can see distant objects at the closest range. By casting gaze one could bring violent animals to total subjugation. We can also put off and put on the lamp. We can move the things on the table without touching them.

Tratak eliminates eye diseases. It removes indolence and neutralises the heat in the brain and thus develops power of concentration.

TYPES OF TRATAK

Mainly there are three types of *tratak*:

1. Near Tratak

We should sit in *sukhasana*[2] and move our eyes up and down as also right and left. The eye tissues get strengthened. The best time for the *tratak* practice is from 4 a.m. to the sunrise.

Place an idol or a rounded white stone at least two feet away and fix your gaze on the object in a deep and undisturbed concentration. You may choose any other object—say a candle flame, nosetip, a piece of cloth or fire or its reflection.

You must continue to concentrate your gaze on the object until tears roll down your eyes. You must not blink your eyes. As tear-drops accumulate in your eyes, you better close your eyes. Ensure some rest to the eyes before you resume practice.

You had better increase the duration of the practice gradually.

---

1. *Dhyana-Sadhana*: Meditation.
2. *Sukhasana*: A sitting pose in which the practitioner sits with his right foot under his left thigh and left foot similarly folded under his right thigh. The head, the neck and the back remain erect and he places his hands on the knees.

On the second day, the practice could be stretched to a longer period than the time you devoted on the first day. When you have succeeded in fixing your sight on the flame of lamp without batting an eye-lid, you should begin concentration with the tip of your nose as the next object. Any prolonged practice with this object is certainly difficult, and yet the benefits from it are immense.

2. Distant Tratak

After he achieves a sound practice of near *tratak* the practitioner must fix his attention on either the summit point of a mountain or a tree top. He may choose the temple-cupola also for this job. After a regular and sound practice, he should take up a more developed practice by concentrating his gaze on the moon. Next he should take up a star for this purpose. Lastly he should make the sun itself as the object.

Initially as you try to fix your eye on the sun, you will encounter total frustration. So the practitioner should practise concentration on the reflection of the sun in water, and then on the looking glass. Finally he should look straight at the sun. If he ultimately succeeds in keeping his eye on the sun for 32 minutes, he may be assumed to have been credited with divine power.

3. Inner Tratak

The first and second types of *tratak* were mostly oriented to external objects. In case of inner *tratak* the practitioner has to close his eyes and achieve practice by virtue of sheer will-power.

He will have to fix his eye on the point between his two eye-brows. In the beginning he will feel considerably baffled. Later as he continues to fix his eye on the spot between the two eye-brows he will begin to see 3 or 5 or 7 dots either bluish or yellowish in shade. After some time the dots will disappear. He will see instead an eye glowing with brilliance. In the beginning the eye will seem to be fluctuating or blinking. He may see in the glow of the eye the sun, the moon and the stars. After some time the practitioner will see the third eye in the sky specially made azure. Next he will see a triangle, dots spreading out at the centre. Even the dots, after some time, will disappear. Thus the practitioner assumes a completeness.

There are certain important regulations which the practitioner must bear in mind. The duration of the *tratak* practice should be extended rather gradually. In order to achieve success through the techniques of *tratak* one should continue to practise each technique for at least thirty-two minutes without blinking one's eyes.

The practice should be discontinued if the eyes begin to water or get tired. Better he closes his eyes and gives them rest for some time.

Unless otherwise stated, *tratak* should be practised either in Sukhasana or *Padmasana*[1].

Precautions

The *tratak* practitioner must abstain from all kinds of intoxicants, particularly alcohol, smoking, etc.

Such persons as are suffering from heart diseases, tuberculosis, leprosy and gonorrhoea should not practise *tratak*. The persons having poor eye-sight are also forbidden.

The practitioner must bear a sound moral character. He must have full control over passions such as anger, sex, etc. He should exercise restraint on his food intake. A light meal will suit him in particular.

The practitioner must sit regularly in the *padmasana* sitting style.

Practise this technique preferably in the mornings. The place should be neither too dark nor unduly illumined.

Soon after attending to the morning chores, the practitioner should start his practice.

One must be dressed in loose clothes.

The practitioners who have poor sight are strictly forbidden to practise the *Surya tratak*[1].

In course of practice if the practitioner finds his eyes going

---

1. *Padmasana:* A classical meditative pose in which both legs are folded and the feet placed on the opposite thighs. The soles of the feet remain upward and the heels touch the pelvic bone.

watery, he should suspend the practice. He should resume only after a long rest.

FURTHER CLASSIFICATION OF TRATAK

The practitioner will succeed only when he has a perfect knowledge of *tratak*. We have already told our readers that there are three types of *tratak*:

1. *Near Tratak*
2. *Distant Tratak*
3. *Inner Tratak*

Near Tratak is subdivided into the following classification: (a) Idol Tratak, (b) Light Tratak, (c) Nose-tip Tratak, (d) Red Cloth Tratak, (e) Point Tratak, (f) Reflection Tratak, (g) Fire Tratak.

Similarly *Distant Tratak* is subdivided into the following classifications

(a) Scene Tratak (b) Star Tratak (c) Sun Tratak.

CLASSIFICATIONS OF NEAR TRATAK

a. Idol Tratak

Take an idol[2] roughly 3 to 4 inches high and put it at some distance. Fix your eye on the idol and start developing concentration. If you do not have an idol, take a picture instead. Make sure that the picture is not coloured.

With the idol or picture before, you start fixing your gaze on the eye of the idol or picture as the case may be. You must concentrate your gaze at the pointed object without least deviation or disturbance. It must be a one-point gaze. You should not deflect your eye unless you feel your own eye watering. At this stage you better take rest for some time. After taking sufficient rest you should close your eyes and bring forth the idol or picture in your vivid imagination and then put it to *tratak* practice. At least 20 or 25 times you should

---

1. *Surya Tratak:* A description of this type is given in the following pages.
2. *Idol:* In India the vogue is to have *Siva-Linga*. This expression means the phallic symbol of Lord Siva, one of the three principal Hindu gods and who is primarily entrusted with the task of destruction.

bring forth the idol or picture in your imagination. After a regular practice spread over a few days the practitioner will be able to bring forth in his imagination the idol or picture without slightest delay. Initially the idol will remain in his concrete imagination no more than a minute or so. Gradually the practitioner will find the idol staying in his imagination for a longer duration.

In the beginning your mind's eye or visual imagination will see many things in addition to the idol or picture. Gradually it will settle down to a one-point concentration on the specific target. Again, this concentration will give the practitioner the power to see any event or thing or person, should he desire to see. In order to see these desired objects, the practitioner should bring tratak to bear on such objects, in addition to the idol or picture. He should try to visualise them as long as possible.

This practice paves the way for the opening of the third eye. As one closes one's eyes and brings *tratak* to bear on the idol placed before, the process of the opening of the third eye begins to assume shape. By this practice the ganglion supporting the third eye gets strengthened.

In Tibet they dig a whole into the head and open the third eye. However, the *tratak* technique has been found to be more effective.

b. Light Tratak

You could begin to practise *Light Tratak* only when you are quite sure that you have successfully concentrated upon the picture for at least 32 minutes.

Light a bigger-size candle and place it in a room secure against strong minds. The idea is that nothing in the room should put the candle-flame off. Now darken the room. Sit on an *asana* at least 3 feet away from the candle. Fix your gaze on the candle-flame. Ensure that no other thoughts or feelings cross your mind.

As you go ahead with your regular practice you will find that the light emanating from the candle is getting more brilliant and dazzling. If you yet continue the practice you will see the faces of many people in the glow. At times you will see the faces of the persons of your choice as soon as you remember them.

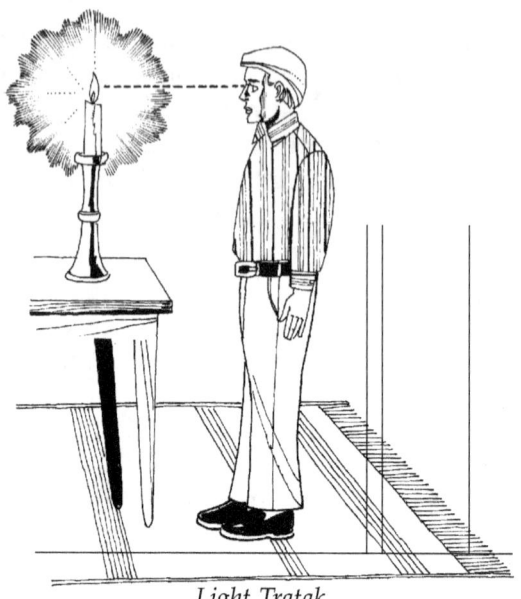

Light Tratak

For real, good results you should practise *Light Tratak* for at least 20 to 25 minutes daily.

In real terms the candle flame is a miniature of fire. For this reason, if you continue to practise this technique, your eye will develop a glow of fire and also such a dazzling resplendence that none will dare look at you. If at all he looks at you, he will find himself rather weak and dispirited.

The Hindu scriptures are replete with real life stories in which the indignant *sadhu* merely looked at the bird seated high above on the branches of the tree and brought it down dead. In a way it was the fire which emanated from his eyes, which eventually burnt the bird.

The practitioner should exercise his power for better ends, and never for ulterior motives.

c. Nose-tip Tratak

You must ensure that you have had a regular practice of *Light Tratak* before you set out to practise *Nose-tip Tratak*.

Begin this exercise by fixing your eye on the tip of your nose. After you have been able to achieve this fixation, you take your eye to settle down at the centre between the brows.

It is a pretty arduous exercise. It gives rise to recurrent headaches. The eye-lids grow painfully restless. So the practitioner should continue to go ahead with this practice and keep on prolonging the duration of the practice. It may be achieved in a day or a month. At times it may take a whole year.

The practice involving concentration on the mid-centre between the two eyebrows is also called *Trikuti*[1] practice. When the practitioner succeeds in sustaining this kind of practice for 32 minutes, he is credited with Divine sight. He can very well peep into the past and see beyond into the dim future. He can also fathom the thoughts and feelings of others. He can see before himself the events happening at distant and obscure places. He can also easily concentrate and meditate upon the image or concept of God.

d. Red Cloth Tratak

Take a square piece of blood-red silken cloth six inches long and six inches wide and stitch it at the centre of a piece of white cloth. Fix it on the wall. Make a point in white colour at the centre of the blood-red cloth. Now fix your eye on the white point.

While practising keep your mind totally subdued and perfectly controlled. As you continue to gaze at the white point you will see the blood-red cloth turning into blue. The white point begins to shine. As you achieve a total concentration, the white point will be invested with a dazzling brilliance. Sometimes it may also vanish from sight.

One can have a similar practice by placing on the red cloth a coarse grain.

When over a long and regular practice the red turns into blue, it should be taken as a pointer to your perfect success. For the blue reflects the inner light of the practitioner.

The practice links the inner mind with the outer mind. As a result many divine ideas come up before the mind's eye. With closed eyes you can see distinguished *sadhu* and *yogis*, as also the scenes of rivers and mountains. It helps enrich the power of memory, too. It eliminates tension. Time loses its dimension.

---

1. *Trikuti:* Named after a three-peaked mountain of the Deccan.

For instance, an hour spent in the practice does not seem longer than a mere ten minutes. In order to avoid the pain of the over-strained eyes, one should not practise this *tratak* more than 10 times a day.

e. Point Tratak

Point Tratak needs a regular practice. At the end of the exercise you better wash your eyes with cold water. It will remove the fatigue. The practice should not be resorted to in dazzling light. Early dawn makes a very suitable time for the practice. If at all one has to practise it in the day time, one better does so in a closed room.

Put a black dot on a large art paper. Affix it on the wall opposite. Squat at a location two or three feet away from the wall. Now you fix your eye on the black dot.

After some time the practitioner will not see the black dot. Instead a dazzling light will seem to have replaced the black dot. When you see a thing like this, take it that your efforts have been crowned with success.

Now introduce a change in the practice. Draw a circle around the black dot in black colour. Now, once again, fix your eye on the black dot. Gradually the practitioner will see that the black dot as also the black circle has vanished. It has been replaced with brilliant lines sprouting about. Again it is an indication to your success as a practitioner.

Introduce another change. Draw seven similar lines around the black dot. Ensure that the black dot remains at the centre of the lines.

Now fix your eye on the black dot. Gradually the practitioner will begin to feel that the black dot as also one or two circumferences does not seem to be present at the same location. As he goes ahead with the practice he will find that all seven circles have disappeared. It means you have already entered your *Turiyawastha*[1]. It is a delightful state, because the seven lines disappeared only when your own inner light blazed forth. The inner splendour gets reflected on the paper with such extraordinary power that the black dot does not appear to exist. The black circumferences around the black dot also do not seem to exist. The brilliant and golden light which you find in its place is nothing but your own inner light which having been reflected on the paper gets into your eyes. It is reckoned as an outstanding achievement.

Now you have to advance to the next higher stage of this practice. Take a piece of white board or white art paper. Draw at its centre an inch-diameter black dot. Gradually the practitioner will find the big dot thinning down. A time may come when the enormous dot may disappear altogether. Indeed for some time the big dot will remain unseen. But gradually it will re-emerge from the small dot it was to its original enormous size. Decrease and increase in the shape is an indication of the success in practice. The decrease indicates that your outer mind is getting dormant and the inner mind activated. Similarly when the dot begins to assume its original shape, it implies that your outer mind is, again, getting activated and is being restored to its original state.

As already explained, when the inner mind gets activated and the outer mind goes dormant, the implication is that the practitioner has reached his inherent state. Now, in this state, he can see distant objects as easily as he sees the objects close by.

Once as I was practising *Point Tratak* I heard footsteps on the stairs below. At that time I was watching that the shape was decreasing in size. In other words, my outer mind was reduced to a dormant state and my inner mind got briskly activated. As I heard the footsteps I began to feel as though the professor of the Kanpur College was arriving, and his name was such and such. I also felt that he was bringing a paper and that certain particular happenings were jotted down on the paper. My inner self had seen into those happenings.

As soon as the stranger was inducted in my room, I told him that he was a professor of Kanpur College and his name was such and such. I also told him that he had brought along with him a letter from an acquaintance of mine and that the letter was in his pocket. There were, I further told him, five questions written in the letter. I told him the specific questions too.

1. *Turiyawastha:* The most engrossing state of spiritual trance.

71

Perhaps the readers will find all this totally amazing. But then, with eyes closed, I was looking at the expected professor, his position, his college and also at the letter in his pocket together with the questions written out. The contents of these questions were revealed to me by my inner mind. And the fact is that I had never met him before.

Such experiences are not uncommon for those who practise this particular *Tratak* technique regularly. At that time the inner mind reaches its full consciousness and so it spreads out all over the universe like ether. As a result he can see all phenomena in their true colours. If a professor comes across the roused consciousness, the inner mind sees through all happenings in the professor's life in original colours. In a state like this if the practitioner wants to peep into the past of the professor, it will reveal itself in its original colours. Much in the same way if he wants to see beyond into the professor's future, the entire future will come out alive.

The fact that the black dot on the paper is shrinking and then enlarging is a pointer to the perfect success being achieved by the practitioner. It makes it perfectly clear that the inner mind being roused to consciousness is able to see what is not possible in normal circumstances. A further change in the dimensions of the black dot suggests that the inner mind is relapsing into a dormant state and the outer mind is gaining back its consciousness.

f. Reflection Tratak

One practises this *tratak* with the help of a large mirror eight inches long and six inches wide. Fix it on the wall. Take your *asana* at least three feet away. Make sure that the room is not unduly lighted. When you look at the mirror you will find your face reflected in it. Now you fix your eye on the mid-centre between the brows in the reflection. Gradually you will not be able to see the reflection. You will see merely the mirror. Now at this stage breathe in at a low speed. The lower the breathing would be, the sooner the reflection will vanish. After some time the reflection will again be visible. Once again if you look at it steadily it will vanish.

You will have to practise like it for about a month. You need not recite any *mantra*[1] while practising this *tratak* technique. When you continue to practise this technique you will start seeing in the mirror many new scenes. If you see a multiplicity of scenes you can take it you are successful in your practices. The implication is that all our suppressed desires and the scenes consigned to the obscure unconscious come out in the mirror through the medium of *tratak*. At times we come across many such sights which have never taken place to our knowledge. But these must have been seen by inner mind. Precisely this is the reason why they emerge in the mirror.

Later as you continue to practise, the sights will disappear. For the conscious mind pervades all over. In a situation like this whatever and wherever it sees anything, it turns out to be a reflection of itself (the inner mind). This state of being is called *Turiyawastha*.

The mirror we have used for such exercises should not be put to any other use. When the practice is over, we should cover the mirror with a fine cloth and keep it safe and secure.

This technique produces a glow in the eyes and soon a spiritual lustre emerges in the sight. By virtue of this lustre one can easily be hypnotised. Even birds and animals get hypnotised. Having cultivated this lustre once you look into the eyes of anybody, he will feel obliged to follow your wish whatever it is. For instance, if you give a look at an incensed person, he will calm down. Even violent animals will act up to your behest.

Even inanimate objects are not outside the purview of hypnotism. Take, for instance, the case of a handkerchief or ring. Give it a steadfast look and suggest to it that whoever looks at the owner of this object will be hypnotised. Little wonder that anybody doing so will find himself totally hypnotised.

Once a friend of mine came to me and said that he was to call on his superior officer the following day. He had committed a blunder. He was certain he would be fired by the superior officer.

---

1. *Mantra:* Any esoteric hymn recited in prayer to God.

I gave him heart. I took away from him the ring he had on one of his fingers. I went to a lonely room and suggested to it whoever looked at this ring would come under the influence of its owner.

I gave it back to its owner. He came back to inform me that the officer was highly furious and he had decided to fire him from service. But the moment he looked at the ring, he calmed down. He let him off with a mere warning.

You can hypnotise any object such as handkerchief or ring. The benefit will go to the user of the object. The hypnotic influence lasts for three months. But if the hypnotised object comes to be washed earlier the influence will go.

As already discussed the *tratak* technique of this kind can influence even birds and animals. Sitting in my garden when I choose to ask a bird perched high above on the tree to come down, it will immediately come down and without the least hesitation start pecking at corn on my palm. Experiments like this have been successfully made on a variety of birds including peacocks. Once a mere gaze at a furious bull brought him to normal.

This *sadhana*[1] transcends time. A long practice of three hours would appear to be a fleeting experience of a couple of minutes. It implies the practice instils in us a sense of pure delight.

g. Fire Tratak

Of all the *tratak* techniques already described, the *Fire Tratak* technique is not only the best, but the most difficult too. Ordinary house-holders are advised against practising this *tratak*. One who has come to gain a total control over one's sexual urges, can practise it successfully. But in no case should this practice be resorted to without the supervision of a teacher.

On a dark night go to a distant forest and collect three or four wooden logs. Put them together and burn them. As flames start rising high, withdraw yourself to some four or five feet away

---

1. *Sadhana:* Meditation.

and fix your eye on the flames rising high. Follow this practice for an hour. Keep a reserve stock of wood so that whenever the flames weaken you can replenish the stocks.

After a month-long practice the practitioner will mark that the red flames will disappear and in its place a glorious lustre will emerge. In this light he will see pictures of many kinds of gods, *yakshas*[1] and *gandharvas*[2] At times we come across sights which we read about in the *Gita* and other scriptures. Practising this technique I myself saw the Mahabharata war as described in the *Gita*.

In no case shall we come across demons and witches. *Tratak* is a God-oriented meditation.

The human body is made of five elements: ether, earth, air, water and fire. The *Fire Trarak* removes from it two constituent elements, viz. earth and water. By virtue of the *Fire Tratak* the practitioner brings about a blending of the remaining elements and enters the universe of the three elements. All gods are made of only three elements. One has to leave behind the two elements named above. It is only then can one reach supreme godhood.

The principal use of the *Fire Tratak* is that one gets endowed with power to enter such realms which are generally obscure and forbidden. The human being who is made of five elements will not be able to reach the universe made of only three elements. He may be the greatest *yogi* belonging to the highest order. Dropping two elements is central to the job of acquiring power to enter all realms of the universe. Until the process of elimination is consummated, one has to remain confined to the mundane framework. One can achieve this only through the *Fire Tratak*.

It was through this technique that I came across many accomplished *yogis*. I saw quite a few of them whom it was otherwise difficult to see. With the help of this technique one sees the remote life in the caves of the Himalayas.

The other important feature of this technique is that as you will be busy practising, a host of accomplished *yogis* will keep

---

1. *Yaksha:* One of a class of demigods.
2. *Gandharva:* Demigods proficient in music and war.

on hovering about you. Their principal job is to render you all assistance.

Sub-divisions of Distant Tratak

We have already discussed the *Distant Tratak*. It is important that one studies its sub-divisions.

a. Scene Tratak

Begin the practice of **Distant Tratak** with *Scene Tratak*.

Better get up early in the morning and after attending to the morning chores proceed straight to the forest. Precisely when the sun is rising, fix your eye on the top of a tree. Practise *tratak* on the tree top. After some time you will stop seeing the tree and its top.

You will see all around only the sky. You will see as if your body has grown pretty light and is floating all over the sky at a terrific speed. At the same time you also see all those sights which are vividly described in the Hindu mythologies.

In this state you will lose all consciousness of your physical dimension. You will enter the transcendal world. Now you will start remembering the past incidents. You will be able to go wherever you might want to go. For instance, in a state like this you may like to visit the Mount *Kailash*[1] and have the worshipful view of God *Mahadeva*[2]. You will feel as though your body is floating and that the Kailash Mount is situated much below your body. You will be able to see Lord *Siva* and His consort *Parvati*. Whatever you see at a time like this will alone be reckoned as real.

After achieving success in this practice, you will be able to concentrate on any person real or shown in a picture. You will be able to gain control over him. For instance, after this practice, if you bring *tratak* to bear on some woman, she will immediately feel subjugated to you. She will carry out whatever order you may like to give her, regardless of the fact whether she is already known to you or not.

However, the practitioner must not indulge in unethical acts.

---

1. Mount *Kailash:* Situated in Tibet and held sacred by the Hindus.
2. God *Mahadeva:* Lord Siva.

b. Star Tratak[1]

There is a limit to our sight. We will not be able to see anything beyond this limit. The star is situated far, far away. So it is not possible to see the star with normal vision.

However the practitioner could fix his eye on a particular star at night. He should continue the practice. He must make sure that the star does not disappear from his view.

After a few days' practice he will feel that the star is getting more visible day by day. He begins to see such sights in the star as were normally not visible. At times the star will disappear from the view and later come back to the view.

The practitioner must go ahead with this kind of practice for about four months. Any place we would like to see comes before us in all vividity. Suppose the practitioner had not seen the Qutab Minar of Delhi at any time. Closing his eyes when he begins to meditate on the Qutab Minar, it will emerge before him in all vividity.

I have had many similar experiences. One day while practising this technique I began to wonder, what my friend Yashawant was doing. When I closed my eyes I saw he was undressing at the tank. I could clearly see his full physique, the tank and the clothes heaped on one side.

I myself reached the tank at about the same time. I found him in the same clothes at precisely the same place. As I had seen in my vision he was taking bath in the tank in the same manner.

After this practice the practitioner can see any event taking place thousands of miles away. When the U.S. President Kennedy was gunned down, some accomplished *sadhaks* who were putting up with me informed that they saw the gunning down in all vivid details.

Indeed this practice is very significant, for it helps see such events as take place far, far away.

c. Sun Tratak

---

1. *Star Tratak:* For the sake of convenience one can first practise gazing at the moon. It should be easier for him to concentrate on the star later.

It should be practised by those who have mastered the techniques of *Fire Tratak* and *Star Tratak*.

To begin with you start the *Tratak* practice by fixing your eye on the rising sun. It may be difficult to stare in the beginning directly at the sun. You could, therefore, begin the practice by gazing at its reflection in the water. Next you start gazing at it in the mirror. At this stage you can look at the sun directly. The duration of the practice should be increased gradually. It could be increased up to thirty minutes. Finally you can fix your eye on the mid-noon sun. But it should not be for more than 5 to 10 seconds in the beginning.

I know a few *sadhaks* who can practise *Sun Tratak* for ten minutes. The person who can practise this technique for as long a period as 32 minutes is indeed blessed with divine vision.

The sun is most powerful. If we bring *tratak* to bear on the sun, the radiance of the sun enters our bodies through eyes. As a result our bodies are affected by divine grace. Our eyes get so brilliant that nobody will have guts to look at us face to face.

The duration should be increased steadily. If we hasten it unnecessarily it may impair our eyes. If one resorts to this practice without having first mastered *Fire Tratak* and for a longer duration it is likely that one will lose eye sight for good. One must, therefore, be very careful about this technique.

OO

6. HYPNOTIC SUGGESTIONS

In the earlier chapters we have rather very frequently used the expression hypnotic suggestion. Indeed in the field of hypnotic science suggestion plays the most important role. It is through hypnotic suggestion that one achieves hypnotic control and the 'subject' is experimented upon in the way the practitioner desires.

Man is an intellectual being and today he has reached the pinnacle of success in the field of science largely through intelligence. To achieve progress in the field of science he has studied, and brought under his control, nature. He has begun to realise that it is more important to study and comprehend the human body. He has also discovered that his knowledge of the human body has been little. The subject has unlimited potential. The more one tries to delve deep into this science, the greater will be our achievements. God has patterned this physique in such a way that every atom remains ever mysterious. It should be, one has begun to realise, an outstanding achievement if we begin to comprehend the extraordinary complexity of the human body.

As one began to ponder deeper, one came with dazzling achievements. One of the mysteries revealed during the exploration of the human body is that it contains certain elements which are felt and yet are not visible. The existence of the mind, for example, is felt beyond doubt, but it cannot be located even after dissecting the entire body.

After extensive researches in this field we have come to know that the human body contains not a single entity known as mind, but two minds outer and inner. When we are awake, the outer mind remains active and experiences every thing. With the help of the intellect, it takes decisions. However, when it stops functioning, during our sleep, the inner mind gets active and takes over the job such as protecting the body. The outer mind goes dormant.

For example, you are sitting near a fire place. You are wholly lost in your thoughts. Unconsciously your finger is found advancing very close to the fire. And yet as it is about to touch the fire, it resiles. The hand finds itself withdrawn from that zone. Now who made the finger resile from the fire? Surely you did not, for you were totally absorbed in your thoughts and you had not been conscious of the position of your own hand. It was the inner mind which made the finger resile from the fire.

As I have argued in the foregoing, anatomists have not been able to locate the mind, although there are as many as two minds in the human physique. Perhaps they have not been able to come across the mind. Nevertheless they accept that the human body is endowed with mind. It alone distinguishes man from animal.

There is much resemblance between man and animal. Both eat, both sleep, both breathe in and out. Both remain active and both can procreate. And yet man is strikingly different from animal. Unlike man, animal can neither contemplate worries nor can it share the joys and sorrows of other animals. Conversely man does share joys and sorrows of others and contemplate, weal and woe. It is the mind which gives man the capability to contemplate and it is the mind which distinguishes man from animal.

The inner mind has, therefore, been very crucial to the human life. For whatever it feels remains enduring, besides eliciting a quick reaction. To take a commonplace example, you tell a healthy friend of yours that he looks sad and that his face has gone pale. And you also suggest to him that he looks already sick and perhaps he is on the verge of falling sick.

His inner mind will accept your words in the same way as these were meant. His outer mind will, however, appear to contradict whatever you have told him. It will appear to explain away the words arguing that you must have uttered these words carelessly. It will argue that the man is not at all sick. But in any case the inner mind is quick to suggest that the face must indeed be looking pale. He must have marked the paleness before he said so.

If what you told him is repeated by two or three more persons, the inner mind will accept the full import of these suggestions and he is brought under its impact. He will begin to feel as if he is actually sick. Whatever he does on that day makes him a little more tired. Perhaps weaker and more depressed. All this must be attributed to the functioning of the inner mind.

On the contrary, you are terribly sad and depressed on a certain day, to take another example. Just at about the same time a jolly good friend of yours drops in. It makes you cheerful, your face brightened up with cheer. Your voice will be sweet and cheerful. Even your intonation will be so soothing you will feel a lot healthier than before.

I have tested this happening many a time. A person of my village was said to be endowed with miraculous powers to cure any scorpion-bitten person. The village folks shared this belief. I personally saw him treating such cases. The scorpion-bitten person would be presented to him. He would recite a few mantras rather incoherently for two or three minutes. He would also rub the affected part of the body in the hard way. The part would go red. And in a matter of three to four minutes the scorpion-victim would start feeling less pain and he would go home cheerfully.

One day as I became very intimate with him, I asked him: 'Could you tell me what is the mantra you recite while curing your patients?' The answer which I got was pretty shocking. 'Mantra' he said, 'No mantra at all. In fact when the scorpion-victim comes to me, I smite at him in the foulest language!' He added that he himself was rather surprised that the patients felt cured all the same.

Later he confided that the pain was not eliminated because of the *mantra*. It got cured because they came fully sharing the belief that he was a profound *tantric* and removing such pain was for him a mere child-play. The mere suggestion removes the pain. In fact, the inner mind accepts that the witch-doctor has a proven capacity to drive off pain by a mere touch of his fingers. So it is not the mantra, but the suggestion which causes its removal.

Mostly physicians fail to locate the ailment in the complex human organism. But the inner mind does not fail in this respect. It locates and removes the ailment.

It is the thinking of the inner mind which is the base of the functioning of the hypnotic suggestions. Just as the inner mind can reach any obscure part of the body, similarly it can travel up to any esoteric part of the world in a matter of a few seconds. In a moment it travels thousands of miles and sees the person at farthest places. Take, for instance, a person who is living abroad. He contemplates his wife and children or anybody else back home. In a second they emerge in front of him. The implication is that as he thought of his kith and kin, the inner mind reached them. Might be his eyes were closed then. He begins to feel what the inner mind sees.

Just as the inner mind can see persons sitting at far away places, it can also suggest to, or command, a person to do a certain job. It needs a special type of practice.

What is needed is that the inner mind is brought under the control of the outer mind. Generally it is not under the control of the outer mind because it has a speed which is both terrible and enduring. However, following a special technique of practice, if the inner mind is brought under control, one can see amazing results. Normally under hypnotic influence we develop the capacity to see wife or son sitting far away. In other words, we see only such sights or such persons whom we had seen earlier. If the inner mind is brought under perfect control, one should be able to see even such sights as one had never seen before. Controlling the inner mind we could see any event taking place in any corner of this world.

Not that we shall develop the requisite capacity to be only passive spectators. We can also intervene in the event. For instance, a friend of yours who is residing miles and miles away can be influenced. With the help of the inner mind you can see him. At the same time if the inner mind is under your control you can make him do anything you may desire.

Now the important question is: How do we gain control over the inner mind? The only answer is: One can achieve it with the help of hypnotic suggestions.

It is basically hypnotic suggestions which give us the strength to bring the inner mind under control. It is by dint of this mind we can have anything done. The concept of hypnotic suggestion may apparently look pretty simple. In reality, however it is very difficult to achieve. It needs a very arduous and regular exercise. It is only after repeated practice that we can bring it under control.

Broadly the human body has three invisible parts—the inner mind, the outer mind and the intellect. You need a perfect co-ordination among them. The outer mind does not accept any suggestion easily. Characteristically it argues. However, the inner mind accepts every suggestion very easily.

Take an example. Go to a patient and tell him that he is no longer ill. His outer mind will not accept it. He will hit back: 'You are wrong. I have not recovered. I am suffering from a terrible headache. My joints ache. How do you say that I look healthy?'

Meanwhile a physician arrives and tells the same patient that he is hale and hearty. The outer mind would feel like arguing that he is not yet recovered. But the intellect would have the upper hand. For the intellect has presumed that the physician is an expert. He knows more about physical ailments. His opinion must be more authentic. When the intellect suggests like this, the outer mind will come round to the position that it is now doing fine. When the outer mind has accepted, the question of the inner mind does not rise. For it always accepts suggestions unquestioningly.

The role of the hypnotist is identical to that of the physician referred to above. It is already known that the outer mind goes by whatever the physician suggests. It is only for this reason that the intellect intervenes. Much in the same way the 'subject' must have full confidence in the hypnotist. Unless the 'subject' has an implicit faith in the hypnotist, neither the outer mind nor the inner mind will accept any of the suggestions made by the hypnotist.

To take an example, the hypnotist suggests that you are getting sleepy. It is likely that your mind counters by arguing that no, the 'subject' is not at all feeling sleepy. In this case the mind intervenes and overrules the objections. Having implicit faith in the hypnotist the 'subject' accepts that he is feeling sleepy. When the outer mind comes under influence, the question of the inner mind does not arise at all. In a situation like this, the outer mind is rendered totally inactive, and the inner mind gets activated and follows the suggestions as sought to be made.

When the outer mind is quietened or put to sleep the inner mind reaches loftier heights and gets further activated. When, for example, you sleep at night, your outer mind falls asleep. Correspondingly the inner mind jumps into activity and starts travelling to long distances. You begin to see the sights through the medium of dreams. These dreams are nothing but what your inner mind has seen or is seeing.

Neither time nor space has any meaning for the inner mind. In a moment it can travel thousands of miles. Similarly it can go into the past and see happenings taking plea several years ago. It can also see into the future—into a happening in the immediate future or remote future.

The incident which you come across in the dream may come true one of those days. You will be amazed to note that the incident reveals itself in real life much in the same way as you saw it in your dream only a couple of days ago. There is nothing amazing about it, for the inner mind had seen the imminent incident. You remembered it.

A situation like this develops only when the inner mind is not under your control. We will have to see all such things as the inner mind sees. On the contrary if the inner mind is under your control, you will see through its instrumentality only such sights as you yourself might want to see. Suppose you want to see when and where and how a certain person would marry, the inner mind would at once take hold of his wish and you would be able to see that he marries at a certain place, he marries a certain girl and all that. It is possible only when the inner mind is under control. In our scriptures this vision was called *Divya Drishti*[1].

Many times as we keep contemplating a very dear and near person, we suddenly find a particular aspect of that person flashing before us. Suddenly a woman feels that her husband who is abroad has been taken ill. She had not worked up any suggestion nor did she practise any meditation. She is upset. Soon she receives a telegram informing that her husband is ill. How did she have the hunch, she wonders. It is not uncommon to have a presentiment if you have gained control over the inner mind. A controlled inner mind can reveal both the past and the future.

The instrument which brings the inner mind under control is hypnotic suggestion. It is only through hypnotism that we can know the full meaning of the hypnotic suggestion.

Without hypnotic suggestion we cannot have the hypnotic process made perfect. Following this process the hypnotist can hypnotise others as well as himself.

HYPNOTIC PASSES

Hypnotic passes are certain movements caused by the hypnotist. The purpose is to hypnotise or dehypnotise a 'subject'. It means that we can extend to others the power vested in us.

In the foregoing pages we have already discussed how Dr. Mesmer proved that every person is endowed with animal magnetism. It can be passed on or transferred to other human bodies. We have also discussed that the power is inherent in every person and it can be further enriched. This exercise involves a regular practice. We have to make use of *shakti chakra* for this purpose. We can make use of *tratak* too. Once we have a regular practice of the *chakra* or *tratak*, the magnetism inherent in us gets such a boost that we can hypnotise anybody in a single moment.

When an accomplished *sadhu* touches a patient on his forehead, the patient gets much relief. It is nothing but magnetism which he got from the *sadhu* through the instrumentality of his fingers.

When you enrich magnetic power in your person, through the medium of *tratak*, you can pass it on to others. It is this action which is known as Hypnotic Pass.

To accomplish this capacity you make a 'medium' sit in front of

---

1. *Divya Drishti:* Divine vision.

you. You are to transfer your animal magnetism into the body of the 'medium'. So keep standing in front of him. Spread your fingers and stretch them as far as possible. Now fix your eye on the fingers and suggest to yourself that the magnetic power inherent in you is flowing on to your fingers. After a short while, you will feel a sort of sensation in your fingers. If you continue to repeat the same suggestion for some time, you will feel a similar sensation overtaking your whole body. Particularly the eyes and the fingers will feel the sensation rather sharply. When you feel the sensation sharply in your fingers, put the fingers on the forehead of the 'medium' and suggest to him that the magnetic power inherent in you is flowing on to his body through the instrumentality of your fingers. Also suggest that the 'medium' is drawing the power and so his body is feeling sensation all over.

After some time you will feel totally quietened. The sensation is gone. You begin to feel lightened. The meaning of this change is that the portion of the magnetic power which you could spare has gone into your 'medium'.

Once again if you want to pass on to the 'medium' magnetic power, you will have to go through a similar exercise. By following this kind of transmission, that is, extending your own magnetic power and passing it on to others, you can make anybody totally free from diseases. You can also give him divine vision. In the Indian philosophy it is called *shaktipat*.

The 'medium' following this operation can derive all such benefits as hypnotists have.

The initial attempt for passing on magnetic power roughly takes 10 to 15 minutes. One should not have more than 2 to 3 exercises a day seeking to pass on magnetic power to others.

After assuming this power one can really reach the exalted status of a spiritual teacher. He is come to be endowed with full power to transfer to his disciple all his knowledge and power.

OO

7. WILL-POWER

Human life is a conglomeration of limitless desires. Man is prone to diverse and many desires. He is ever busy trying to fulfil some of his desires. The desires which get fulfilled are also a source of great pleasure for him. And yet there are some desires which go the way of all flesh.

Often he longs to fulfil his desires and on good many occasions he longs to fulfil the desires of other persons. He derives a particular type of pleasure as he seeks to fulfil the desires in others. And yet there are such compulsive desires in his own life that he does everything to fulfil them. When he is unable to achieve his desires he is overtaken by a strange unrest.

Man is always tormented by a host of desires. The shallower we are, the greater the number of desires. If we want to have some control over desires we must have a ruthless control over our mind. This can save us from many troubles and obstacles. At times, to fulfil a petty desire we expend a sizable portion of life. When the desire is at last fulfilled we do not derive as much delight as we thought we would.

We should try to control all kinds of desires. We should organise all kinds of stray and multitudious desires into a collectivity and try to bring about sublimation of this entity. The better we organise our desires, the greater will be our spiritual, social and physical integrity.

I have already argued that we feel tormented due to a plurality of desires. It is because of an innate shallowness that we harbour all kinds of desires. The pressure is such that often we lose our mental balance. It is essential that we got over the shallowness ingrained in us. Now we are slaves to desires. Perhaps, in that case, desires will be slaves to us. We shall be able to make use of them in any manner we choose to do.

There are several types of people. Some people have no strong will-power, with the result that they are overtaken by desires and they become slaves to desires. Desires in multitudes keep on haunting them. They are also lacking in self-confidence. As a result they do not succeed in fulfilling their desires. Their life is reduced to one of imbalance and abject tormentation. On the contrary there are some people who have a strong will-power. They are the people who can control the strongest desires. Such people suppress with an iron hand all such desires as are harmful and anti-social. They seek to fulfil only such desires as are significant socially. Through this medium they serve the society and join the celebrated.

Those who are weak-willed are always controlled by voluptuous senses. They are left with no self-confidence. They keep on hankering after their desires. They live a slow life. They do not have high aspirations. If at any time they do have such high aspiration, they brush them away, weak-willed as they are.

In order to achieve integrity and superiority man has to develop a certain strength to control his desires. It is only by controlling desires that man has achieved what apparently was wholly impossible. He has been able to conquer the Himalayan summit; he has been able to cross the Sahara desert and the vast and frightening expanse of the oceans. Looking at the impossible feats he has achieved, it is not difficult to know how he has been able to do so. It was sheer will-power which got him whatever he wanted, whether possible or impossible. To this end he bent all his energy, crushed all other desires and worked hard. He cared a fig for all kinds of dangers in his path. True he did encounter many obstacles. But he was certainly not overcome. He never accepted defeat. The moment any other desire came up, he suppressed it. He had one very clear-cut target and he advanced with a single-minded devotion to that end.

What is basically important is that we should have an objective recognition of our own capability. We should know what we are lacking in. What are the factors which have made our life so common and mundane and how we can bring our thoughts and mind under control.

It is essential that we are strong-willed. Unless we develop a certain measure of volition we shall not be able to succeed in any job. Whenever we take up any job it is likely that we are confronted with certain difficulties and obstacles. If we are not strong-willed we are likely to give up the job. So with a sense of determination we should plan out the job well in advance. When we start doing the job we should be determined to complete the job, come what may. We should not develop any weakness or slackness until the job is accomplished. It is only by will-power that we succeed in life.

Scientists have found out that our desires are closely related to our breath. Every breath gives rise to desire. The more we breathe in, the greater the number of desires. So if we do not breathe in as much, we shall not have so many desires in life. The most authentic and effective way to control our breathing is *pranayama*. It is by effective control over breathing that the *sadhus* and other accomplished meditators achieve a total control over their desires. Besides, they have a strong will-power which enables them to suppress contrary and mundane desires.

In order to cultivate a strong will-power it is essential that we are physically strong and healthy. We can achieve a strong health only when we are free from desires. Otherwise these lowly desires eat into the vitals of a strong and healthy constitution.

How does anxiety get germinated? It is due to our efforts to do what is socially and ethically reprehensible. Whenever we have done such a job we try to keep it a secret. A fear that it will be out reduces our body to an unsuspect hollowness.

Life should, therefore, be balanced. First we must not do anything which society does not approve. Suppose we have done a thing like this, we should not suppress it. To err is human, and so we must be more careful about committing mistakes in future.

How to enrich will-power?

A strong will-power is crucial to success in one's life. It is by virtue of a strong will-power that one can suppress one's desires. There are some methods following which we can achieve for ourselves a tension-free and strong-willed mind.

1. You get into a closed room. It should have a dim light and also a soft music. Ensure that as you are practising this method, nobody knocks at the door or puts any obstacles

in the way.

Put off your clothes and stretch yourself on the bed. See that your body feels relaxed. Now you suggest to yourself that your feet are totally relaxed and so they are unable to do anything. Now you suggest to other limbs one after another—such as waist, heart, chest, stomach and hands—that they, too, are feeling relaxed. In none of them is any action being noticed. Last you suggest to your mind that it is also feeling relaxed and it has no desire or thought. Finally you suggest to yourself that you are feeling drowsy and perhaps you are about to fall asleep. In a couple of minutes you will drop asleep.

This experiment has a tremendous significance. Every limb follows whatever you suggest. Even the brain if suggested goes thought-free. The entire psyche is at your command. Thus you come to possess total control over your mind.

2. If at all you have contracted a bad habit or tendency you put it down on a piece of paper. And place it somewhere so that it can always hit your eye. Your writing table, for instance, can be an ideal location. Say you are given to chain-smoking. You tried hard to get rid of it, but you could not. Now you write on a piece of paper: 'Come what may I shall not smoke from today onwards,' and place it on your writing table. Suggest to yourself that your psyche is quite capable and you can have control over itself. You will not smoke in any case. You suggest to yourself 3 or 4 times a day. Whenever the urge to smoke is taking an upper hand, you look at the table and suggest to yourself that you will not smoke in any circumstance.

At night before you retire for sleep suggest to yourself that you will not smoke. Whether you develop headache or tension or indolence, you stick to your determination.

If your determination remains as it is, you will certainly give up smoking. It will be taken as an indication of your will-power getting strengthened day by day. It will give you a lot of pleasure too.

3. Put down any five lines from a book in front of you.

Have a timepiece. Now take a vow that you have got to commit the five lines to memory in only ten minutes. Now repeat the lines without uttering them loudly. Suggest to yourself that you have got to learn them in ten minutes. You yourself will feel that you have learnt the lines within ten minutes. As you continue with this kind of practice, reduce the time progressively—from 10 minutes to 8, from 8 minutes to 6, so on and so forth. Soon you will reach a stage when you can learn any five lines in no more than a minute.

4. Ascertain what time you take to cover a certain distance on your bicycle. Suppose you negotiate a distance of 2 kms in 10 minutes. Now you start progressively reducing the time-duration. While you will not feel tired or panting for breath, you will certainly be able to negotiate the same distance in reduced time.

5. You start counting in reverse from 1000 to 1. Ensure that you do not take more than 10 minutes for this job. You take a firm decision that you will now do reverse counting only in 8 minutes. If you achieve this feat taking even less time, it should be taken as an indicator of your firm will-power.

You are to bear in mind that you will do a certain thing taking less than the allotted time. It will show that you have gained full control over yourself.

You can have another interesting practice. Place a timepiece in front of you. Fix your eye on it, being seated at a place without the slightest movement. At least for 10 minutes continue to watch like this. During this allotted time even if a fly settles down on your face, you shall not budge an inch. In other words you may have any kind of obstacle, but you must have grim determination to stick to it in any case. Your determination must know no relaxing.

If you go about the job with sustained determination, you will achieve it within the allotted time-span.

6. After having accomplished the practices referred to above, the practitioner should take up bafflingly difficult jobs or such jobs as normally take a very long time.

The practitioner should take up a difficult job which takes at least a month. In that case, he must accomplish the job within a month.

Similarly the practitioner should fix up to have a certain income within a certain period. Whatever difficulties he may have to face, he must earn this amount within the time schedule.

It is likely that one has to face many difficulties and obstacles doing a job within a fixed time schedule. Whatever be the difficulties he must not give up. If he has full control over his will-power, he will certainly achieve it.

Vibration in Will-Power

As we have already discussed, we have in the human body two minds—outer and inner. When the individual is active, his outer mind remains conscious and inner mind is less active. But as soon as the individual falls asleep, the inner mind gets more active and he begins to see such sights as he had never seen before. Dream is the sequel of the travels of the inner mind.

Base of Hypnotism : Vibration in Will

All consciousness and active objects of the world vibrate. Vibration is crucial to all of them, whether it is air or sky or voice. Vibration gives rise to waves. As a result the waves help move from one place to another. When you speak, the waves of your voice travel outside. As a result others hear your voice. For the sound-waves hit the ears of the others. The louder you speak, the farther your sound waves will travel.

Similarly if your will-power remains strong, it must have its impact on others. A strong will-power has a far-reaching impact. On the contrary a weak-willed person hardly creates any impact of any range.

Today it has been proved beyond doubt that one can send out one's strong will-power to a distance of thousands of miles. One can also take under one's impact any person living thousands of miles away through sheer will-power. Once he is exposed to the assault of your will-power, one can have anything done at the other end.

So it is axiomatic that, given a strong will-power, one can create a pervasive impact upon objects thousands of miles away and bring any person under one's influence. To test this enunciation, you could work out one or two experiments. Make a friend of yours residing in your own town your 'medium'. First you get into a solitary room and lie down on the bed. The room should have a dim light. Now relax your body. Close your eyes. Work up your friend's face and see it face to face. Ensure your eyes remain perfectly closed.

Now suggest to your friend's face that it help itself with a drink or light a cigarette on its own or do anything on its own as suggested. Suggest like this to the face at least 6 to 7 times.

In order to ascertain the impact of your suggestion, you better phone up your friend and ask him what he did a couple of minutes ago. Indeed if your friend reportedly had a drink or smoked a cigarette on his own only a couple of minutes ago, you better take it that your experiment has borne fruit. Do not feel put off if you have not succeeded in the first attempt. If you have not succeeded even after repeated attempts, the snag must be somewhere with your will-power.

Eventually when you have succeeded in making a friend of yours living in the same town, you shift your focus on such of your friends or relations or acquaintances as are living in some other town. Being seated in your own room you suggest to one of them that he better phone you up this minute or set out to see you.

You will notice that your suggestion will have its impact on the person located far away. He will be getting ready to act up to your suggestion. Indeed unless he does so, he will be feeling upset to a degree.

Similarly you can plant the suggestion in your adversary that the cause of enmity is being withdrawn from this day and so he must restore cordial relations with you. A friend could be suggested that he has developed intense feelings for you and that without seeing you he cannot have any peace.

Several experiments of this nature could be resorted to. You can test your will-power through such experiments. True, the job is initially very arduous. True, it may take a long time. But there is no earthly reason as to why you should give it up midway and feel frustrated. You may rest assured that you will succeed, although you may fail in your initial attempts.

After you have succeeded in such experiments, you are not to sit back. You should rather go ahead with more arduous experiments and try to achieve miracles. For instance, you can down a flying bird. You can put off flame without going near it. You can stop a speeding train.

Our history records similar achievements in a good number. There is nothing miraculous about it. No witchcraft sustains it either. The whole thing could be attributed to your own strong will-power. Given a strong will-power you can achieve impossible things.

To further develop a strong will-power, we suggest the following steps:

1. As a rule, speak less. The more you speak the greater will be the wastage of your energy which is inherent in your body. In that case you will have to work a lot to get back your lost energy. So the best course is to preserve the energy inherent in your body.

2. As a rule, do not keep the company of illiterates, idiots and the weak-willed. They are the people who inject in us pessimistic feelings. They have been failures in their own life. They want to see others failing similarly. Keep away from such elements.

3. Spend a part of your time in profound solitude. Nobody

will talk with you and nobody will put any obstacles in your way.

4. Do not reveal your thoughts or secrets to anybody. If you feel incensed, try to gain control over your anger. Even in a laughter provoking situation, try to restrain yourself. You shall not laugh. It will ensure self-control.

5. One who has a proven confidentiality about oneself gets a higher place in society. If you share some of the secrets of your friends or acquaintances, you will not disclose whatever be the provocation. Suppose the relations at one stage cool off, and yet you will not betray confidence. You must sustain a mystique about yourself. The more you do so, the greater will be the honour.

6. Put on an expressionless face. Suppose somebody is telling you what he considers as top confidential. Perhaps you already know it. And yet you must not betray on your face any expression suggesting that the top secret is not a top secret. Put on such an expressionless face so that he is convinced that you have come across this top secret for the first time.

7. Do not try to show off by dressing in any uncommon way. You should dress yourself in a common way. If you appear to be unique, you will not be able to mix up in society at large. You will not be able to inspire confidence if you do not dress up as the society generally does. No hypnotist will be able to succeed in his art unless he enjoys the confidence of the broad sections of society.

8. Try to make your mind thought-free. We have already explained the method in the foregoing pages. Consolidate the achievement by repeated experiments. It will create on your face a divine glow. It will give you a necessary balance. It will enrich your memory. The brain will be stronger. Undesirable thoughts will be hounded out. Only desirable thoughts will remain in your mind.

9. We have already discussed that the eye is the chief instrument of the hypnotist. It is through the instrumentality of the eye that he seeks to hypnotise somebody. Practise *shakti chakra* to be able to look steadfastly at a given object

for a long time. This will enrich your eyes with a special kind of magnetic power. The 'medium' will have no other way than to succumb to your power.

Following these methods the practitioner must bring his will-power under his control. It will be a signal achievement in his life. He will be able to succeed through this medium.

OO

8. NYASA DHYANA

Of all the methods recommended all over the world for the purpose of elevating standards and achieving balance in life the *Nyasa dhyana*[1] is the most significant. Through the instrumentality of *nyasa,* one can identify all vital centres of one's body. At the same time he can heighten his awakening through these vital centres.

The following 26 are the vital centres provided in the human body:

1. Soles 2, 2. Calves 2, 3. Thighs 2, 4. Genital Organ 1, 5. Navel 1, 6. Heart 1, 7. Lungs 2, 8. Shoulders 2, 9. Right palm, hand & shoulder 3, 10. Left palm, hand & shoulder 3, 11. Eyes 2, 12. Ears 2, 13. Mouth 1, 14. Nose 1, 15. Eyebrows 1. So the total is 26.

In one's life the process of elevation takes place only through these vital centres. It is, therefore, essential that one recognises one's body and also the 26 vital centres embedded therein.

True we know a lot about these centres and yet we do not reflect over them. When, for instance, we are busy we just do not bother about the vital centres referred to above. It is only when certain events are caused that our mind turns to these vital centres. Now a nail gets stuck up in one's sole, which makes one sit up and sharply realise that the sole is a vital part of the body. Otherwise we just do not worry about the sole.

I should like to say with all emphasis at my command that we should certainly not live a life of normality. We should rather pay regular attention to all the vital centres of the body. It is but natural that a particular limb being not properly cared for would go inactive. Earlier I discussed that several centuries ago man had in him a certain active ganglion. With the aid of this ganglion he used to look into the past and peep into the future without any extra effort. But as he got embroiled in mundane activities and overlooked cultivating this ganglion, it became gradually inactive. It stopped doing even the normal job it was assigned with.

Even today this ganglion is very much in the human brain. Medical scientists have identified it, but the ganglion has been reduced to inactivity, although it continues to be alive. Similarly if we do not pay attention to, and cultivate, the 26 vital centres provided in our body, one reasonably fears that some of them, if not all, may become inactive, although they will remain alive. In that case we shall not be able to continue to derive benefits from all centres. I would, therefore, urge readers to pay attention to these centres at least once a day so that they remain active.

---

1. *Nyasa Dhyana*: The literal meaning is act of taking care of or looking after. In *yoga* it is a system of *yogic* exercise in which controlling of respiration is practised. *Dhyana* means meditation.

More than any other limb the human mind is engrossed in external activities. As a result it does not bother to pay any attention to these centres which are embedded in the inner system. Should we choose to activate the inner mind at least once a day and pay proper attention to all these vital centres, we will certainly grow healthier. Besides, man will be able to restrengthen these centres by ensuring a proper circulation of the *pran shakti* provided in the body. In such case, he will feel healthier. He will get rid of diseases. Above all he will have a better strengthening of the *pran shakti*. As a result he will develop his magnetic power, which will ensure a more successful life.

In the foregoing pages I have already discussed *nyasa*. More often than not, it is easier said than done. But I am quite certain that the practitioner will be able to free himself from many besetting problems if he succeeds in learning the experiment of *nyasa*.

For instance, you have a shooting pain in the head. In a matter of seconds you can get rid of this nasty pain if you know how to make use of *nyasa*.

In the following lines I should like to give an outline of the method of *nyasa* as it is largely practised.

When he sleeps at night and gets up in the morning the practitioner should put on loose clothes. Now you stretch yourself straight on bed. Drop the body quite loose and relaxed. The body should be left so loose that you may feel your body has no strength left in itself. You should neither blink your eye nor allow any limb to go active. This posture is called *Shavasana*—the posture of the deadman.

Now bring your breath under control. Exhale whatever air you have in your lungs. Gradually pump in fresh air. You will have a delightful sensation as you do so. Make sure that you are breathing slowly.

After this you rouse both your internal and external minds all at once. In other words, concentrate with fullest devotion on all the 26 vital centres provided in your body in the order as given in the beginning of this chapter. For about 20 seconds keep chanting the *Mantra*[1]—'OM CHAITANYA CHAITANYA SWAAHA'. It should be chanted slowly as you concentrate from one vital centre to another. Say you begin with soles and move upward strictly following the order as suggested.

Keep yourself to the same posture. Keep lying on bed. As you chant the *mantra* devoting 20 seconds for each centre, you suggest that the particular centre is getting activated and that a particular consciousness has emerged in that centre.

First you go over all the 26 centres in the ascending order and similarly you move back touching all the centres in the descending order. Thus you have completed one sequence.

You must practise it regularly. In a few days you yourself will realise that a special kind of energy is overflowing your body. You will feel more enthusiastic and more active. The magnetic power natural in you is also developing. A particularly attractive halo has set in on your face and you influence all people sooner than expected.

Many and diverse are the benefits accruing from the practice. Your body as a whole gets a special type of respite. It will re-strengthen your cells. You will get back sleep if you are suffering from insomnia Besides, the *pran shakti* which is gaining in power will spread out extensively touching all parts of your body. As a result all parts get activated. They help one another and help in the process of the entire physique. At any rate it should be taken as a signal achievement.

The practice eliminates all chronic diseases such as indigestion gastric disorders, anemia, gout, headache, etc.

Whenever you have any physical ailment you lie down in the same *Shavasana* pose. You should concentrate upon the affected part. Suggest to it that the trouble is gone and now there is no longer any pain. In about 10 to 15 seconds the practitioner will feel that the pain is gone and he is freed from the ailment.

You can have this practice at any place you like. In any case, make sure that there is absolute peace reigning about. No

---

1. The *Mantra* should not be repeated loudly.

flies or mosquitoes should hover about. You must be dressed in loose clothes. Take a balanced, vegetarian meal during the period of practice. Empty stomach during practice will help you concentrate on all vital centres for a long time.

I have described the method calculated to rouse all the vital centres of the body. Nonetheless it is not all that easy. One has to encounter various kinds of obstacles:

i) Despite repeated attempts the mind at times refuses to concentrate. At times it concentrates after repeated attempts for no more than half a second.

ii) As we try to concentrate, all kinds of stray thoughts assail our mind.

iii) The method to relax the body is no less difficult. In spite of regular and repeated attempts one finds some vital centre is somewhere active in its own way. Often we do not achieve *Shavasadhana* the way it should be.

iv) When you have achieved concentration of mind and fix it on some object, you will find it slips to some other object. I have suggested that we should devote 15 to 20 seconds centrewise.

The process is very complex and one succeeds only after repeated practice.

v) Many a time the practitioner forgets the order of the vital centres. This failure leads to complications.

vi) The meditation requiring us to concentrate on all the 26 vital centres is time-consuming. Besides, to keep both the outer and inner minds at a single point is very difficult. It is only after a regular practice stretched over a long time that we can have both the minds concentrated for such a long time. We must follow the order as I have already suggested.

vii) At times when the practitioner relaxes his body and having concentrated both the minds brings the vital centres, one after another, under influence he falls asleep. And in the long run when he gets up he forgets everything about it.

viii) When you have completed one sequence, the body finds itself so passive that you fail to get up even after some attempts. In a situation like this the practitioner should allow his body to remain as it is and make it active gradually.

When you have completed one sequence, you will feel much lighter, a strange delight will overtake you and you will feel as though you are floating on high waves.

In the process your mind grows totally carefree and dispassionate. The arteries in your brain get activated. As a result your memory gets strengthened.

While practising, you better suggest to yourself: Whatever I am doing is only for my own happiness or in devotion to God. After all, this body is a gift of God. By rousing the vital centres of the body I am hastening the process of man submerging in God.

Enriched by such lofty thoughts you will be able to succeed in this practice. It will also put the *pran shakti* to a much better use.

Now I propose to discuss all about *dhyana*. We have already explained the importance of *nyasa* in a practice like this. *Dhyana* is no less important. If we succeed in settling our mind at a certain point, it is likely to have a profound and pervasive impact all around. It is like a pitcher containing as many as twenty holes. Water will gush out through all these holes. If the pitcher has only one hole, water would have gushed out through that solitary hole only. In the pitcher with twenty holes the pressure gets fragmented while in the other pitcher the pressure does not get fragmented. So the velocity in the latter case will be greater.

The human mind works exactly like the pitcher. If there are twenty desires or thoughts, the pressure gets fragmented. In a state of being like this, suppose you bless or curse anybody. The impact coming as it does from a fragmented source will not be as pervasive. But, once we concentrate the entire mind to a single thought or target, it is bound to have a bigger impact on the target.

The ancient *rishis* had perfected this method. They used to concentrate all their ideas or tendencies on a single object. So a curse or blessing said by such ancient persons was bound to have created a far more extensive impact.

Dhyana is nothing but a means to bring one's mind under total control. If you stop for a moment and start reflecting you will find you are unable to prevent a host of thoughts crowding about in your mind. In other words, when we cannot control our mind for a single minute, how do we hope to gain control over the mind during long, sustained practices?

It, therefore, involves a long and one-point practice. For one cannot hope to achieve anything without controlling one's own mind. In the Indian *Yoga* system, a number of methods have been suggested to achieve control over one's mind.

TECHNIQUE 1

Stretch yourself on a cot, or on a thick cushion on the floor. Close your eyes. You must try to concentrate your mind. No hurrying up and no impatience. It is only when you devote some time that you would be able to bring about the desired concentration of the mind.

When you are able to concentrate, bend the forefinger of your right hand. While doing so, ensure you absorb yourself in this job with all your senses and sensibilities. No other thought should cross your mind. Bending of the forefinger is the one-point concentration to which you must make everything else subordinate.

Now choose the middle finger to bend. You must ensure the same concentration, proceed to bend the remaining fingers, while ensuring the same mental concentration.

Repeat this exercise on the left hand following the same pattern.

Now take up the job of unbending the fingers in the same order as you bent them. As you straighten the forefinger, you must have achieved a total concentration on the single point of operation. Proceed to the next finger and so on and so forth. Take your own time. A deep and one-point mental concentration is the principal object.

Do not be impatient at any stage. You may repeat the practice 5 or 6 times a day in order to accomplish the initial mental concentration.

TECHNIQUE 2

Stretch yourself on your back on bed. Ensure that the bed does not have pillows or sheets. Stretch both legs in a straight posture. The left hand must remain parallel to your body, while the right one should spread out as far as possible.

At this stage you slowly allow the body to relax. Now suggest to your inner mind that your own right hand should rise above and settle down on your chest. You shall not indulge in any distraction. No other thought shall ever cross your mind. You yourself will not raise your right hand.

On the contrary what all you are to do is to simply suggest to your inner mind. Whether the inner mind follows your behest as soon as you have suggested, depends on the mental concentration you have obtained.

You will see that your hand will by itself rise high and gradually lodge itself on your chest.

Now, at this stage, you can take to another experiment. Suggest to the inner mind that you are feeling chilly. In a few moments you will see you will feel perfectly chilly and you would look about for some blanket to cover yourself with.

Better repeat this kind of exercise twice or thrice a day.

TECHNIQUE 3

Stretch yourself on bed. Concentrate upon a single sentence. You may, for instance, take the sentence—'God is one'. As you contemplate the sentence, ensure you are applying total concentration and that you are not allowing any other thought to cross your mind. Keep on contemplating on this single sentence with nothing else to distract your attention in any manner.

The concentration must in any case be absolute. As you are practising somebody may walk in. The criterion for your concentration is that you should not have heard his footsteps. It is a certain indicator of your concentration now absolutised.

Gradually, you should increase the practice. It will develop your inherent mental capacity to fix your concentration at a single point.

TECHNIQUE 4

Take to this practice preferably when you retire for sleep at night. Lie down comfortably on bed and close your eyes. Now, you recapitulate what all you did that day—right from morning when you got up until the time you have retired for sleep at night. You are to recapitulate all jobs in the order as you did. You recapitulate, for instance, that you got up in the morning. Your left leg touched the floor or the right one. You got into the bathroom. What did you first do there? Then you went to office. Who did you come across first in the office? What did he say? How did you confront him? Who else met you? What did you eat in the lunch? Try to remember literally everything whatever your wife told you. You also try to remember, whatever you told your wife.

You must recapitulate the day's activities from morning to night in the same order as you did, each one of them. The order must not be disturbed.

The first sign of your success is that you can recapitulate all activities of the day. Try to increase this practice. After a few days you will be able to remember all activities in the same order without much effort.

Now you may try to recapitulate whatever you had done, say, the previous day. Go back as far back as possible.

Indeed the practice is pretty arduous. However, it will ensure a sound concentration of the mind. The more you do it, the better.

TECHNIQUE 5

Broadly this technique is complementary to the fourth technique. Stretch yourself on bed as you retire for sleep at night. Close your eyes. Try to recapitulate who you first came across, when you set out from home for office the previous day. Who did you see first? With whom did you talk first? What was his apparel? What did he say to you? What you said in reply, try to capitulate word by word.

When you advanced, you came across a car. What was its

number? How many persons were seated in it? When you still advanced you saw on the left many buildings. What sort of buildings were they? Did you see any particular thing on the right side? Was some particular person standing by?

Try to recapitulate in the same order. This practice is somewhat more difficult than the previous one. But you must devote yourself with some application. You will succeed.

It has a rare significance in one's life. For instance, you just give a look at a given page of a certain book. You will remember the contents without having to read it again. One may quote you any number. There may be any numerals in it. And yet you will remember it.

This method ensures an absolute concentration of the mind. It has its own delights too. When, for the first time, you set out from home for office, your outer mind was wandering elsewhere. True, your legs carried you, but your mind did not notice the persons who crossed you on the road. Even if you saw them, you did not retain the image. Thus you retained not a single image, for the mind had strayed elsewhere.

Now, your mind will remain particularly awake and vigilant. It will take note of all persons carefully and try to retain the images.

TECHNIQUE 6

No doubt this technique surpasses all others in its complexity. However, a regular practice will ensure all success.

This method is called mind-worship. After having gone through his morning chores including bath the practitioner should sit down on his *asana*. As he slowly closes his eyes he should try to obtain an idea-free mind.

Now work up before you the image of the God you worship. Work up the image to emerge in front of you. It must appear to stand before you in bold contours. No other idea or distraction of any sort should be allowed to cross your mind. In my own case I look at the image in as real a form as its animate incarnation is normally viewed. I devote all my worshipful attention to the image. I bathe it. I dry it in soft silken cloth. I dress it up in colourful attire. I decorate it using the purest objects. I lay at its feet colourful flowers. I shower on the image a bath of scent. I put a light in front of the image. I place flowers and fruits as we normally do as part of worship.

All these jobs I do while sitting on my *asana*. The entire job takes half an hour, if not more. I derive a particular delight doing this worshipful job.

Nothing crosses my mind at that time. The object is before me. I see only the object. I also see the various ingredients of worship. I see the same sight as I do in a temple dedicated to my God. I chant a particular *mantra* in worship. My *mantra* has been: OM GAM GANPATAYE NAMAH.

I gave vivid details of this worship only to drive home that the practitioner achieves through it a rare capability. He develops a rare strength to entertain only such thoughts as he would like to do.

As you read these lines, you might presume that this exercise is not as difficult as is being suggested. It is indeed very difficult. It needs a regular practice spread over a long time. This meditation is of a high order. It has immense benefits. The ingredients give us not only physical benefits. The light you offer to your god spreads out an inner light within you and even within the people who might be sitting outside. The flowers, the scents and all other ingredients of worship send out a spiritual fragrance which spreads over all people both inside and outside.

It gives you a particular satisfaction. When I offer food to my god, I derive a particular delight.

Subsequently when I bring my concentration to bear fully on the image, I do not find the image any longer. I see the god himself in all his majesty and magnificence. I see his brooding eyes and smiling lips. It is a rare sight the distance between the devotee and the god is abridged. In a way the devotee finds himself totally submerged in his god.

This is the ultimate stage of this meditation. You can reach a still higher stage. In the total submission you have achieved, you can obtain more than one body of yours—say two or three. You must suggest to yourself that you cannot have a full, integrated view of your god with the help of only one body and the two eyes provided in it. It is, therefore, necessary that you should reorganise yourself in two or three bodies. You will feel astounded to see that you have in your place two or three bodies, each body trying to have a worshipful view of the god.

This meditation gives you the strength to assume many bodies. You can remain seated at a given place and send out another body of yours to distant places to see and talk with somebody. The other body does what all your own body is capable of doing.

I will explain this point by offering an instance from my own life. In the scriptures it has been said that one gets immense spiritual benefits if one offers the water of the *Gangotri*[1] in the temple of Lord Siva at *Rameshwaram*[1]. A few year ago I had been to the *Gangotri* alongwith my wife and other family members. I brought a pitcher full of the sacred *Ganga* water to offer it to Lord Siva at *Rameshwaram.*

Busy as I was with manifold activities, I could not go to *Rameshwaram* this year. So I sent my wife and son to *Rameshwaram* to offer the sacred *Gangotri* water to Lord Siva.

Precisely at about the same time I had a guest at my residence —Hari Om Baba. Downstairs in a room I was meditating. The Baba was also seated on *asana* close by. The other members of the family were my daughter, my younger son and my daughter-in-law.

One day as I sat for meditation and hardly two minutes must have elapsed when the Baba suddenly got pretty disturbed. He had known that my wife and son had gone to *Rameshwaram.* He rushed upstairs and called my daughter Saroj. He said: Child! daughter-in-law (he referred to my wife) has gone to *Rameshwaram.* Please find out whether she has left the pitcher behind.

Saroj went in and found that her mother had left the pitcher behind inadvertently. The pitcher stood at the usual place in the oratory. The Baba said: Okay. Get me the pitcher. Poor daughter-in-law—she is seated just now in front of the Lord

---

1. *Gangotri:* The source of the sacred Ganga river, situated up in the Himalayas.

and repenting for the lapse Saroj handed over the pitcher to the Baba. He took it and rushed out. Saroj had seen him going to the wall surrounding my house. In about 7 to 8 minutes he came back without the pitcher.

He resumed his seat in the room. He was panting heavily. He was sweating all over his body. He seemed to have run a long distance.

I said: Baba! What is the matter? Why are you panting?

He said: Indeed old people have to run if they have children like you.

The Baba continued to pant. I felt baffled to see him in such a condition. He added: You have sent daughter-in-law and child to *Rameshwaram*. The pitcher has been left behind. There the daughter-in-law being full of remorse was repenting for the lapse. So I had to reach it to her.

In the evening Saroj told me that the Baba went out alongwith the pitcher. She had seen him going upto the compound wall. She had also marked him carrying the pitcher. He came back in about 10 minutes. He was without the pitcher.

I could see the entire process. I myself was in meditation. The Baba was mentally free. So he could see into the repentence of my wife through *agam sadhana*. With the aid of *Vayavi Vidya*[1] he physically went up to the *Rameshwaram* temple and handed over the pitcher to my wife.

The next week when my wife and son arrived at home, my son took no time in recognising the Baba. He said: Mother—it is this Baba who brought us the pitcher.

My wife recounted the whole story: When I reached *Rameshwaram*, I found that the pitcher had been left behind. With a heavy heart I reached the temple and broke into tears before the Lord. As I was repenting, I heard somebody calling out. My son rushed to the door. A Baba stood there with the pitcher. He said to my son: Give it to mother. Tell him Narayan

---

1. *Rameshwaram:* A pilgrimage situated at the Southern tip of the Indian peninsula.

has sent it from Jodhpur. When my son gave me the pitcher I felt delighted. I myself went out to see the Baba. He had meanwhile left the place.

The Baba gave a simple smile. I told my wife and other family members all about the Baba—particularly how he gave me company in deep forests and on pilgrimage to Mansarovar.

What is this *Vayavi Vidya*. It is nothing but an organised form of the practice referred to above. What I mean to say is that the practitioner can have similar extraordinary effects if he continues to have a regular practice of this meditation. Sitting at a given place he can assume several bodies and make his many bodies visit to many places all at one time.

There are other benefits, too. If he continues to have a regular practice he will have an ecstasy truly divine in nature. When he submerges himself in God, he imparts unto himself certain elements of Godhood. For the devotee and God establish a perfect identity in one undivisible whole. The devotee like God will exude a special kind of fragrance.

On mental plane you will become one with Him. Your body will exude *ashta gandha*[1] which is nothing but divine fragrance.

One should not be surprised that the bodies of many sages and uncommon Yogis exude this fragrance. It is all due to this kind of meditation.

---

1. *Vayavi Vidya:* A kind of mental meditation.

9. THE STOICAL MIND

The explorations we have made in the preceding chapters indicate that the mind is centrally important in the human body. Through the instrumentality of the mind we accomplish such jobs as seem to be difficult, if not impossible.

As established earlier, the outer mind is by and large accountable for the normal functioning of our life. On the other hand, the inner mind which is stronger by all means, is wholly accountable for man's conquests in the realm of divine perfections. For the purpose of hypnotism the inner mind is the chief instrument.

We have also discussed that the mind is always active and normally it is never devoid of ideas or thoughts. And yet, given a bit of effort and regular practice, we can certainly make the mind idea-free. To achieve a state of mind like this will certainly be a very big accomplishment. By obtaining an idea-free mind we can ensure a measure of respite to the mind. At the same time, we can use it as an instrument to concentrate all our mental faculties on a certain object. When we are able to make the mind concentrate all attention on a certain idea, the velocity of the mind takes a sharp upturn.

Generally a mind such as this is called stoical mind. The practice to achieve this kind of mind involves Yoga meditation, particularly the following methods, and *pranayams*.

TECHNIQUE 1
Stretch both hands. Stand for sometime with both hands stretched straight. Ensure that both palms face the floor. And the hands are straight. Now you breathe in slowly. Finally breathe out slowly.

TECHNIQUE 2
Stretch both hands straight. Keep standing for a while. Now

---

1. *Ashta Gandha:* An assorted perfume of the following eight fragrances: *tagar, dhoop, chandan, malayanil, veerochan, veerupaksha* and *rakta-chandan*.

slowly move your hands to your head. When the hands go upwards, breathe slowly. Pump out all air stored in the lungs with all force at your command. Note that you must exert yourself while breathing out. On the other hand when you breathe in, you should do so slowly.

TECHNIQUE 3

Spread out your hands in front. The two palms must face each other. The fingers should remain open. Breathe in quickly and then breathe out slowly.

TECHNIQUE 4

Keep the two palms facing each other. Keep them facing your chest and interlock the fingers. Exert utmost and breathe in. And with the same force breathe out.

TECHNIQUE 5

Interlock the fingers of both hands. Throw up your hands into the sky as high as possible. Now breathe deeply. Slowly and steadily breathe out.

The five techniques described above seem to be very commonplace. But they have a special importance. It regulates breathing and we succeed in regulating our breath. Needless to say, a controlled respiration also controls the incidence of the rise of ideas in the mind.

∞

10. HYPNOTISM

We have already given our readers an introductory knowledge of hypnotism. But now the readers must have realised the importance of hypnotism in life.

Hypnotism strengthens will-power, besides ensuring full control over the mind. When the hypnotist succeeds in controlling his own mind, he develops the capacity to control the minds of others also. Hypnotism emancipates us from bad habits and intoxicants.

There is a lot of misunderstanding about hypnotism in the ranks of people. Some people understand it as no better than witchcraft. And yet there are others who view it as an outright anti-social knowledge. They argue that taking resort to hypnotism we achieve only our ignoble personal ends. It is a black art, they conclude.

Such arguments put to a deeper reflection are wholly illusory. Indeed hypnotism is a complete science in itself. Like other sciences it is oriented to do good to people.

Any science whatsoever can be put to good and bad uses. Take for instance, a knife. You can cut vegetables with it. You can tear apart a human being using the same knife. The knife itself is quite innocent. Everything depends on the person who makes use of it or who abuses it.

The mind is central to the art of hypnotism particularly the stoical mind. In order to achieve much in this knowledge and gain integrity in its learning it is essential that we control the mind and also succeed in making it stoical. If we control our own mind, we shall be able to control the mind of others.

At the same time, a strong will-power is also very essential. By virtue of a strong will-power, we can have a brilliant glow in our eyes. A celestial shine will brighten the eyes. Through the instrumentality of *tratak* we can achieve impossible tasks.

Take note of the fact that a suspicious mind puts many hurdles in the way. So it is necessary that you have a determined mind. A high degree of optimism must inspire you. You must be confident that you will succeed in whatever you do.

There are certain formulae which every practitioner should keep in mind:

1. Do not allow any doubts or suspicion to assail your mind. You must be positive that you are correct in whatever you are doing. The 'medium' you have chosen can be hypnotised and that you will bring him under hypnotic influence in a few moments.

2. Suppose you are not as yet fully initiated into all the complexities of hypnotism. Nevertheless you should not tell your 'medium' that you are not wholly proficient. He must always feel that he is in the hands of quite a capable hypnotist.

3. Make your voice suave and sonorous. You must choose your apparel tastefully. Your personality should influence others.

4. Instil confidence in the 'medium' and take him into your confidence. You must not mix up very cordially with your 'medium'. There must be respectful distance between you and the 'medium'.

5. If you fail in your initial experiments, do not lose heart. Might be there was a specific factor for this failure. But, in any case, keep up a regular practice. Remember if you lose confidence in yourself, others will also lose their confidence in you.

6. While experimenting you should be careful and vigilant. Every limb of yours—such as eyes and mouth—should remain very active. It will ensure an effective impact on others.

7. While experimenting you must rely on your expertise and capability. You must not entertain even slightest pessimism. You must have rooted confidence that you will succeed in your assignment.

8. You are no less than the biggest hypnotists. You have in you as much capability as they have in themselves. So forge ahead with this confidence.

9. Do not talk irrelevantly. Do not stoop low.

10. Wherever you practice the atmosphere around must be peaceful. Noise and din and bustle must not pollute the air. Until full peace is restored, do not begin your experiment.

11. When the 'medium' is brought under hypnotic influence suggest to him in clear and unambiguous tone. Your voice should not betray any indifference, weakness, diffidence or slackness or loss of confidence.

12. If the 'medium' does not wake up after the course of hypnotism, you need not worry. It is not at all harmful. He might have gone into natural sleep. So when he goes through the full course of his sleep, he will wake up naturally.

If you follow these formulae, you are likely to be an outstanding hypnotist. You will succeed.

WILL-POWER

Earlier we have already discussed a good many points about will-power. We would, however, reiterate that our life is largely determined by will-power. At the same time, we can influence others largely with the help of will-power. A spurt in will- power brings a brilliant glow in our eyes. Will-power has, in fact, been the rockbottom of the science of hypnotism. When we succeed in influencing others with the help of will-power, we develop at the same time a high measure of self-confidence.

The readers, we presume, already know some facts of hypnotism. We will expect that the practitioner will go about practising the first steps as already explained and ascertain how far he has been successful.

To cite an example, a person is going ahead of you. Now you fix your eye on his neck. Remember he is totally unknown to you. Strengthen your own will-power and then suggest to him that he look back at you. If he looks back at you in a few moments, it will imply that you have been successful.

We have already explained that when you store up will-power in you or when you suggest it to somebody you must not feel any diffidence. For the foundation of willpower is the mind. If will-power is assailed by doubts, the mind will not have the force which it should have. Doubts vitiate will-power. If you want to create any impact, it will certainly not come off.

If you work on the experiment quoted above and succeed in it, it is well and good. Suppose you do not succeed, there is no reason why you should worry about. It simply means that you have not been able to strengthen your will-power.

Initially I too had encountered failures. But I did not give up. Whenever I failed I put in redoubled efforts. Thus I strengthened my will-power. With a single-minded determination I would, once again, jump into the fray. Of course, with a confidence that I will succeed in this attempt.

Take the next practice. Choose such a window of your house as opened to the window of the house opposite. Close your own window, but provide a hole in it so that you can peep into what is going on in the house opposite.

Now, whenever somebody is visible in the window opposite, you fix your eye on him and summoning all your will-power suggest to him to do something of your choice. You could, for instance, ask him to look out from the window or dress his hair with a comb or change into another shirt.

Make sure that your eye remains riveted on him. If he does what you have suggested to him, it should be taken as a pointer to your success.

You could move on to the next step. Suppose you are seated in a railway train. In the other extreme corner of the compartment somebody else is seated. Now summon all your will-power and suggest to hint that he should feel restless and come to you to ask for the day's newspaper.

You will see the man will indeed feel restless. He casts his eye about out of restlessness, and then rushes to you for the newspaper.

The meaning is explicit. One should continue to do such practices. For it gives him confidence in his effectiveness.

A more straightforward reason is that your will-power stems from the mind. Since due to practice your mind has gone stoical, the will-power gets further strengthened. As a result when you experiment it on a certain person, you will find that his mind, being not at all stoical, is not that strong. Your inner mind, therefore, dominates his inner mind and he feels compelled to do what you have suggested. Since his inner mind feels dominated by your suggestions, his outer mind, too, feels compelled to do whatever you suggest. This is the crux of the hypnotism effect.

MORE PRACTICES

You make somebody sit in a chair in a room. As for yourself you keep standing in front of him. In any case you are to make sure that he has already come under the impact of your personality. Besides, he must have an implicit confidence in your capabilities.

Ask him to close his eyes. Now summon all your will-power and suggest to hire that his eyes are closed and howsoever he tries he will not be able to open the eyes. Despite your suggestion he will try to open his eyes. He will fail. He will not be able to even move his eyelids.

The reason is very clear. For your inner mind has implanted in his inner mind the suggestion that he has closed his eyes. He will in no case be able to open his eyes, howsoever he may try.

If at all you do not succeed in such experiments the reason for this must be attributed to a certain lack in your will-power. Your success will be commensurate with your ability to make your inner mind idea-free and also with your capability to summon a strong will-power.

After you obtain success in these initial practices you should seek to hypnotise a person. It is only when you have succeeded in hypnotising a person that you will seek to hypnotise more persons.

You better take note that the hypnotic sleep is no less important. In natural sleep one sleeps soundly. He will not respond to what we say. It is only when you prick him with something sharp, he will jump up in utter confusion. He will find his sleep is gone. On the contrary, when we put somebody to hypnotic sleep, his outer mind no doubt goes to sleep. But his inner mind remains wide awake. Again, it will be under the influence of the hypnotist.

So the person asleep hypnotically does answer to the questions of the hypnotist. In natural sleep, however one does not come across such instances.

The conscious mind distinguishes between good and bad. It does, or responds to, anything by virtue of intelligence and wisdom. In hypnotic state, however man is not left with wisdom. He simply follows the suggestions. For instance, the hypnotist tells him that he has beside him a peacock. He will accept the presence of the peacock unquestioningly. If you use 'sister' for the hypnotised man, he will respond as a woman does.

In hypnotised state the individual can talk properly. He replies correctly to the questions asked. For the outer mind, being not awake, he simply cannot tell lies.

The inner mind of the hypnotised man is directly under the impact of the hypnotist. So whatever the hypnotiser suggests he responds to the suggestions uncritically. If there are other people standing about and suggesting to him to do this or that, the hypnotised will not carry out their suggestions. For the inner mind of the 'medium' is directly linked with only the hypnotist.

STAGES OF HYPNOTISM

In the hypnotic state the medium is put to a particular kind of sleep. As a result his outer mind goes to sleep. On the contrary his inner mind remains wholly active and conscious.

In the initial stages of the influence the 'medium' closes his eyes. He feels totally relaxed. There is a simple smile on his lips, which indicates that he is having rest. If he were asked, in this condition, to open his eyes, he does open his eyes. But he does so with some effort. In fact, he enjoys sleeping in such a condition. He feels more relaxed in having his eyes closed. His breathing goes moderate. In this condition whatever you suggest to him he accepts.

The second stage is said to be more profound. In this case the hypnotic sleep goes deeper. His eye balls rise above, hands and feet get heavy, respiration is slowed down and he is unable to open his eyes even after repeated attempts.

While he is in this state of being, you suggest to him that he better keep his hand at such and such place. He will act accordingly. Ask him to raise his hand straight. He will do so, facing no inconvenience in the process.

The third stage is said to be a complete stage. Here one has all those situations which the 'medium' comes across in the earlier two stages. In this stage the sleep of the 'medium' is further deepened and he will not be able to move his body even after repeated attempts.

He replies correctly to all questions asked. He cannot tell a lie, though he may be wanting to do so. He does not remember any of these things when he is restored to his consciousness.

HOW TO HYPNOTISE

On the strength of my own personal experience I must emphasise that the evening is the best time for inducing hypnosis in a person. Calm and peaceful atmosphere is conducive to hypnotic experiments.

Select a beautifully got-up, neat and clean room. Unwanted things must not find place in the room. If it is too hot, the fan could move at a moderate speed. A sweet and pleasing fragrance will eminently suit the practice. Such persons as are given to overtalking and argumentation should be asked to leave the room.

Ask the 'subject' to sit in a comfortable chair. Let him relax every part of his body, particularly hands and legs. Ask him to stretch his hands and legs in a relaxed manner. Also ask him to count from 100 to 1. This will make him sharply alert and help him concentrate his mind upon a single thought viz. reverse-counting.

Now the hypnotist should stand in front of him. The appearance of the hypnotist must be profound and deeply reflective. Ask him to look into your eyes. You must also look into his eyes. As you do so, tell him in a serious and sonorous voice: Look, you are about to fall asleep. I see, rather clearly, your eye-lids are getting heavier. Soon you are going to have a deep sleep. In fact, you yourself want to sleep. Close your eyes. Go to sleep. Sleep! Sleep!! Sleep!!!

You will see as you are suggesting these actions, the eyes of the 'medium' are getting sleepy, and that he is about to fall asleep. Meanwhile you relax sitting in the chair.

Ensure that whatever you suggest should be put across in clear and unambiguous language. The suggestions should be positive and in no case negative.

As far as my experience goes the hypnotist at this stage is likely to commit a mistake. He may not rest assured that the 'medium' has actually been hypnotised and that he has fallen to hypnotic sleep.

The moment the hypnotist's mind gets assailed by such thoughts, his inner mind comes in direct clash with the 'medium', and the clash of contrary thoughts with the inner mind of the 'medium' results in disturbance of the hypnotic sleep. It is, therefore, essential that the hypnotist does not allow any doubts to assail his mind. He must have a total and undivided confidence in himself. If he goes about his job with a single-minded determination, he is bound to succeed.

Now alter this stage when the 'medium' has been roundly hypnotised or has gone to hypnotic sleep, you may ask him any questions or make any suggestions. The 'medium' will not remember whatever suggestions you make or questions you ask until when he will be restored to consciousness. In fact he will not remember anything said or done during the hypnotic state. However, if you tell him in this state he will remember what all you are telling him now, he will certainly remember all such things when he is restored to consciousness.

We would now discuss certain methods of hypnotisation:

METHOD 1

Make the 'medium' sit in a chair comfortably. Take a ball made of glass. Hold it in your hand and spin it atleast a foot away from the 'medium' right in front of his eyes. Ask the 'medium' to look straight at the ball without blinking his eyes.

Now, you tell him that the bait is invested with miraculous powers. Also if he looks at the ball without blinking his eyes, he will fall asleep. Tell him he is sleepy. His eyes have got sleepy. He is losing all control over his body. Ask him whether he heard your voice carefully. Tell him that his hands and legs are now feeling heavy. He finds it difficult to keep his eyes open. Tell him: Okay. Close your eyes. Go to sleep. Sleep! Sleep!! Sleep!!!

METHOD 2

Make the 'medium' sit in a comfortable chair. Ask him to close his eyes. Then press the middle of the two eye-brows with your right thumb. Rub hair on his head gently with your left hand. Tell him: Your head is feeling heavy. You are feeling sleepy. Now you have fallen asleep. You have slept already. Do you hear me? You must listen to me. You must follow whatever I ask you to do.

METHOD 3

Make the 'medium' sit in a chair and ask him to close his eyes. Now, you ask him in a serious and yet sonorous voice to do reverse counting from 100 to 1. And tell him as he would come to the numeral 40 he would feel sleepy and by the time he arrives at the numeral 30 he will fall asleep.

You will mark that he will be put to hypnotic sleep as suggested. By the time the 'medium' reaches 30, he will fall asleep.

METHOD 4

Ask the 'medium' to look straight into your eyes. When he begins to look into your eyes, ask him to close his eyes. Ask him to multiply 12 by 6. And also tell him as he works out the correct figure he will begin to feel sleepy and then slowly he will sink into a deep sleep.

Indeed as the medium goes about concentrating to work out the exact figure, he will fall asleep.

Better take note that the mathematical problem you would like to suggest in such cases should be easy and it should fit in with the education and intelligence level of the 'medium'.

METHOD 5

Place a wooden board at the centre of the room. You could also make use of a square piece of glass. But it should in any case be atleast one foot wide. At the centre of the board or glass piece, whichever you use, put a candle. Make 5 or 6 'subjects' sit around the candle. Ask them to look steadily at the candle. When you find them looking at the flame, suggest to all of them together to close their eyes. Tell them that they are about to sleep soundly. Ask them to go to sleep.

You will see that they have actually fallen asleep. The hypnotist should continue to practise this kind of mass-hypnotism.

METHOD 6

After a sound practice you make the 'medium' sit in a chair or on the floor. In either case he must sit in front of you. With the help of two fingers you close his eyes. Now suggest to him to fall asleep. You will see that he will fall asleep at the very initial suggestion.

HYPNOTIC EXPERIMENTS

With a view to ascertaining how far you have been successful in inducing hypnotic influence, you could test your knowledge with the help of the following experiments:

1. When the 'medium' is already brought under hypnotic influence, you tell him that he is already feeling sleepy. His eyes are already feeling rather heavy. He is unable to keep his eyes open despite conscious efforts. Tell him: You will not be able to open your eyes until I ask you to do so. He will try in vain to open his eyes. He will, however, not succeed.

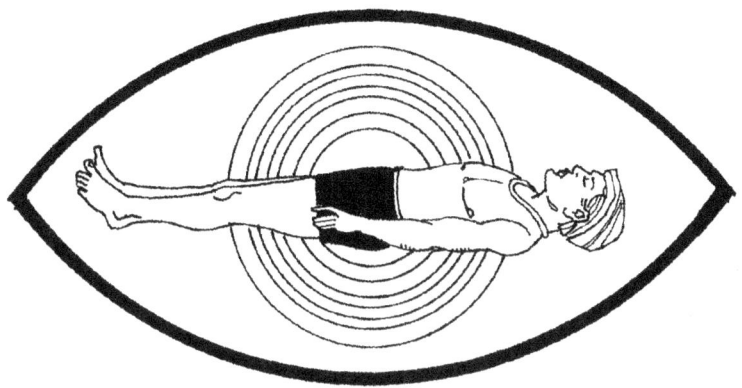

Hypnotism Circle

2. When the 'medium' has been put to hypnotic sleep, suggest to him that he should interlock the fingers of both hands with one another. Now tell him that he will not be able to undo the interlocking despite his repeated efforts. And yet you tell him to undo the interlocking of the fingers. You will see that he will not be able to release his fingers, howsoever he may try.

   Now, at this stage, suggest to him that his hands are gaining in health. He could disengage his hands. The moment the 'medium' is given this suggestion he will break loose the two hands. If he does so, you are to take it that you are getting successful in your attempts.

3. When the 'subject' is put to hypnotic sleep, ask him to stretch his hands and hold them high towards the roof. Ask him to keep on sleeping. Suggest that he will face no difficulty or pain. You will see that the 'medium' raises his hands high above and keeps his hands in the same position although half-an-hour has since elapsed. Now suggest to him to bring his hands down. One thing is very clear. The 'medium' will not bring his hands down until the hypnotist asks him to do so.

4. When the 'medium' has already been put to hypnotic sleep, tell him that you are pushing into his arm a sharp needle. He will, however, feel no pain on that score. When you will

really push into his arm a needle, you will hardly find any pained expression on his face. It is clear that he has not experienced any pain. Such experiments have been found very useful in surgical operations.

5. When the 'medium' is having hypnotic sleep, tell him that he is sleeping soundly. Suggest to him that he will wake up the moment you cause him to smell rose-scent. Now make him smell rose-scent slowly.

   If he slowly opens his eyes, take it that your experiment has been successful.

6. When the 'medium' is having hypnotic sleep tell him that he is sleeping soundly and that you are counting numerals from 1 to 10.

Also tell him that as soon as you strike 10 he will open his eyes. Now count the numbers. In any case you should do so slowly.

If he opens his eyes as you strike 10, you must take it as a sign of your success.

TESTING OF POST-HYPNOSIS ACTIONS

We give below a set of experiments intended to test whether the post-hypnosis actions of the 'subject' conform to your suggestions or not. In these experiments you will speak to the 'subject' who have passed into the first or second stage[1] of hypnotic sleep.

1. Tell the 'medium': Look. I am waking you up. You must eat some biscuits which are in the cupboard soon after you wake up.

   You will see that the 'medium' will feel terribly upset for a minute or so until he opens the cupboard and eats biscuits.

2. While the 'medium' is hypnotically asleep, tell him: Look. I am waking you up. But you are stuck to the chair. You will not be able to get up and detach yourself from the chair. Try to get up all the same. You will not succeed. You are wholly stuck to the chair. Now you open his eyes. You will see that he is unable to get up from the chair. No doubt he is trying hard to get up. But he does not succeed.

It means that the 'medium' is following the suggestions which you gave him during his hypnotic sleep.

3. While the 'medium' is sleeping hypnotically, inform him that his name is Jag Mohan, and that he will remember this name even after he wakes up. Tell him that he has forgotten his real name.

Now, at this stage, wake him up. Ask him what his name is. He will quote Jag Mohan as his name.

4. While the 'medium' is in hypnotic sleep tell him that you are waking him up. Also tell him that after he wakes up, he better rush to the bookshelf and pull out such and such book and open it at page 60 and put it up to you.

The 'medium' will feel restless until he carries out the suggestions, which is a pointer to your success.

5. Show the 'subject' a blank paper. Make sure that you do so only when he is hypnotically asleep. Tell him that the' blank paper contains the picture of some great king, say, Shivaji. Also tell him that he must find out and give you the said picture after he wakes up.

You get hold of four diverse pictures and mix them up with the blank paper. Wake him up. He will examine all

the papers—one blank and the remaining four containing four pictures.

He will give you the blank paper, for he sees only on this paper the picture of the king you showed him. You ask him whose picture it is. He will say it is Shivaji's.

6. When the 'medium' is in hypnotic sleep, fill four tumblers with water and tell him that the tumblers contain soft drinks. Also tell him that when he wakes up, he will have to serve soft drinks to four friends of yours and one to himself.

Now, at this stage, wake him up. Following the hypnotic suggestion he will serve four tumblers to your friends. He will help himself with one and sip from it as one sips soft drinks. To him pure water will taste like soft drink.

The experiments given below should be taken up only after making the 'subject' pass into the third stage of hypnotism. In this stage the inner mind of the subject is made completely free. It can go anywhere along with its subtle body. It can see any happening anywhere on the earth and also report on it.

Time and space are no limitations to the hypnotised person when he has reached the third stage. In a literal sense he gets endowed with powers of clairvoyance.

Once I had to conduct an experiment of this sort. A friend from Lucknow came to me. His son Govind was absconding. He was untraceable.

He was really upset. The boy was his only son.

I chose for my 'medium' a boy hardly ten years old. I hypnotised him and worked him up to the third stage. I asked him to find out where the boy called Govind was at that time.

In a couple of minutes the 'medium' informed that he was putting up with such and such *sadhu* at Hardwar. In fact the same *sadhu* had abducted him. The 'medium' informed the name and address of the *sadhu* and also particulars about his dress. He said that Govind was in great distress at this time. He was being harassed.

---

1. The stages referred to have already been discussed earlier in this chapter.

I hypnotised the 'medium' in front of all others. So they heard the full report and the next morning they left for Hardwar. They spotted the boy Govind precisely at the same place they were told. The *sadhu* was dressed in the same manner.

Similarly I have conducted this experiment on many occasions. Every time I succeeded. You will, however, get the total benefit when you succeed in taking your 'medium' to the third stage of hypnotism.

To cite another example, tell the 'medium' that he must see you at 9 in the morning on Saturday. You deliberately named Saturday, for it would come exactly six days after the day of this experiment.

Now you wake up the 'medium' and take care not to refer to the particular suggestion. You will simply be amazed to see him arriving at your place at 9 a.m. sharp on Saturday. You suggest in his hypnotic sleep after working him up to the third stage that he will have to do a certain thing on a day two months hence. He will appear on that day without fail. Otherwise he remains supremely restless. He will in no case forget the suggestion given to him in the third stage.

1. Lead the 'medium' to the third stage of hypnotism and you yourself stand behind him. Take some book in your hand. A particular chapter must remain open.

   Now you ask the 'medium' to read aloud the lines which you are reading silently from the chapter of the book.

   You will feel simply amazed that the 'medium' starts reading aloud exactly the same lines on which you had fixed your eyes:

   The meaning is simple. At that time the inner mind of the 'medium' was wholly free. It was in a position to go anywhere it liked. It was, therefore, no big task for it to locate the exact lines in the book[1].

2. Lead the 'medium' to the third stage and ask him to describe an event of his childhood which he has not told anybody about in his conscious state. You could, for instance, ask him about a love affair or an act of pilferage or anything one might keep only to oneself.

You will be surprised to know that he will not keep anything to himself. He will tell you everything truly.

3. Having led the 'medium' to the third stage, tell him that he is hopelessly boozy. It is injurious for health. Tell the harm it can do to its addicts.

   Now suggest to him that he has already developed aversion for booze. He must get rid of this nasty habit in future.

   At this stage terminate his hypnotic stage and send him away. Make secret inquiries as to whether he has given up the booze fixation.

   You will be amazed to find that he has developed a perfect aversion for booze. Whenever he looks at booze, he finds it pretty smelly. Even if he might want to have a peg or two, the smell takes an upper hand and he remains away from this habit[2].

4. If you have a person to be operated upon, you hypnotise and lead him to the third stage. Tell him that his leg has to be operated upon. It would involve surgery. But he would have no pain whatsoever. And also tell him that he would not gain back consciousness until you have counted numerals from 1 to 20.

Following this method you can take your own time for the purpose of operation and the 'medium' will wake up only when you have counted upto 20.

One must, however, note that the 'medium' will hear whatever you say. Suppose there are other persons along with you. When they talk, the 'medium' will not hear them, let alone follow their suggestions.

He will get up when you have counted upto 20. Any other person doing the same will not be able to wake him up.

One can thus see that hypnotism, particularly its third stage, has the potential to do immense good to mankind. It emancipates us from all kinds of troubles. The hypnotist can help himself and at the same time help others.

Once the 'medium' reaches the third stage of hypnotism, he can be made to do anything which is in his interest.

We have already made clear that there are some people who cannot be hypnotised. Often such persons are notorious for their hardheadedness, argumentativeness, over-cleverness and wickedness. And yet if the need arises to hypnotise even such persons there are certain methods following which they can be brought under hypnotic influence. It is true beginners will not succeed in tackling such persons. However, experienced hypnotists can hypnotise such persons.

At times it was noticed that even experienced hypnotists failed to bring such persons under hypnotic influence. We would, therefore, like to discuss certain methods to hypnotise such persons.

There are two methods which can be employed to hypnotise such people (i) playing records of hypnotic music, and (ii) making use of an instrument called Matronome.

Hypnotic music records are available in foreign countries. When a certain individual is lying on bed, you can play such records near the bed. As he would hear the music, he would fall asleep. He will be hypnotised. You can now make him do anything you want.

Matronome which is available in India produces a ticking sound. Tick, tick—it produces this kind of sound. It ticks a hundred times per minute. Make the 'medium' lie on a comfortable cushioned bed. Place matronome close to him. You tell him that the ticking sound is meant for him. Every tick means that he must go to sleep. He must concentrate his attention on the tick. He will hear 'Go to sleep', 'Go to sleep' in the ticks being created.

In course of time he will fall asleep. It is hypnotic sleep. Now you can make any experiments whatsoever on him.

Select a dark room for using this instrument so that the red light is visible clearly and affects the 'medium' to a considerable extent.

---

1. Tie inner mind of the 'subject', at this stage. feels quite free. It can go anywhere it likes. It can sneak into the portion of the book being read by the hypnotist, and read out the same lines to him.

2. The third stage of hypnosis offers a sure remedy for drug-addicts. Anybody who is an addict can be helped in this way.

The most appropriate time for this experiment is either evening or night. If you want to have the experiment conducted in day time, you better close the doors of the room and draw all curtains.

As the 'medium' spreads himself on bed, you better win his confidence by talking informally on subjects which generally fascinate him.

You will also ask him to look steadfastly at the glass by facing him, which is fitted on the matronome. It gives red light, and twinkles alongwith the ticking sound.

Tell your 'medium' that the red light is tiring and the tissues of the eyes are made sleepy. He is also coming under the influence of the red light. His eyes are also getting sleepy. He is going to sleep. Now you go to sleep—go to sleep—go to sleep.

You will note that the 'medium' is feeling sleepy. He is closing his eyes. He falls asleep.

HYPNOTISM: SOME IMPORTANT POINTS

1. Any time is good enough for inducing hypnosis, but mornings are better. Evenings are still better than mornings.

2. The room you select for experiments should be a calm and quiet place, free from flies and mosquitoes. The walls should be painted with colours soothing to the eye. A sprinkle of scent all over the room should ensure a sweet-smelling fragrance. It should preferably be a part of the hypnotist's own residence.

3. The lesser the number of persons in the room, the better.

4. Experiments should not be conducted on social and religious functions (e.g. marriages, religious festivals, meetings, conferences, etc.)

5. The hypnotist should not criticise a person who is not susceptible to hypnotic effects. He should rather take him into confidence and gradually bring him under hypnotic influence.

6. Children, weak-willed women, sentimental persons and also such people as having implicit faith in the hypnotist

can very easily be hypnotised.

7. The hypnotist should not use a language not followed by his 'medium'.

8. The hypnotist should speak in an earnest and serious tone affirming his full confidence in his own abilities. In no case should he speak rudely. He must have full faith in the propriety of his hypnotic suggestions or injunctions.

9. The hypnotic suggestions such as made to the 'medium' must not be disagreeable to the customs and practices of the 'medium'.

10. A woman should not be hypnotised at a secluded place lest the hypnotist himself be swayed by feelings of voluptuousness.

11. Insane persons do not make hypnotisable 'subjects'.

12. Patients suffering from hysteria and epilepsy are greatly benefited when exposed to hypnotic influences. On the other hand chronic diseases such as cancer are not cured through hypnotism.

13. The hypnotist should conduct only one experiment at one time.

14. The hypnotist can always rectify his mistakes, if any. For instance, after de-hypnotising a certain 'medium' the hypnotist realises that he has planted a wrong suggestion in his mind. In that case, he should induce in the same 'medium' hypnosis for the second time and plant the correct suggestion.

15. Repeated experiments do not affect adversely.

16. The hypnotist should not make his 'medium' do such actions as may eventually make him a laughing stock in his family and society.

17. Blue colour is most conducive to success in hypnotism.

18. The hypnotist should carry out his experiments patiently and with a steady mind.

19. The 'medium' should have absolute confidence that whatever is being suggested is in his overall interest. It is only then he will follow the hypnotist's suggestions.

20. The hypnotist should have full respect for the sensibility of the 'medium'. Hypnotising a woman he should not ask her to undress. It violates her sense of decency and so her hypnotic sleep will disintegrate.

∞

11. HYPNOTISM IN DAILY LIFE

More than ever man today is bogged up in complexities and difficulties. We are caught up in problems more than necessary and we are encountering problems and pitfalls at every step.

Busy and preoccupied as he is, man finds himself beaten not so much by physical ailments as by psychological maladies. He craves for mental peace. He wants to forget his anguish and his wants for some time. He wants to make his life balanced and happy.

It is hypnotism which has the inherent capacity to solve all these problems. With the help of this science we are in a position to overcome mental distress. Suppose a malady has got into your system which is eating into the vitals of your body. The hypnotist, in that case, will work up hypnosis in you. It makes you ignore the presence of the malady. It can even make you forget all about the malady. There are a number of sorrows which make our life hollow—such as bereavement in the family, insolvency and loss of face. It is, again, hypnotism which can secure us release from these abiding sorrows.

Some diseases particularly mental maladies are taken care of only by hypnotism. It is also particularly useful in surgical operations as also in the treatment of female diseases.

Every moment of his life man suffers from high tension. With tension escalating man grows old prematurely. His face goes pale, without the usual lustre and light. It is therefore very essential that man is liberated from his deepening tension. Again here too hypnotism comes rather handy.

In his personal life man can derive immense benefit. As we have discussed earlier, whatever you think at this moment has its own impact on others. Suppose you are going to see a friend. Your mind is seething with hatred for him. Outwardly you are a picture of love and affection. And yet your inner mind is burning with hatred, which is bound to have a powerful impact on the inner mind of your friend. As a result his inner mind gets as much hateful. It also elicits a similar response from the outer mind. The inevitable result is that he does not feel the happiness which he should have normally felt on such occasions.

Suppose, to take another example, you go to a friend or superior officer for some work. You have a little bit of hesitation. You wonder whether he will oblige you. The doubt which assails your inner mind touches the inner mind of the superior officer. He begins to see into your doubts. As a result, the job is not done.

To take one more example, you approach your boss with authentic documents in support of your application for long leave. At the same time you are quite doubtful. Your doubt infects the inner mind of the boss. No wonder it tickles in him a contrary reaction. Your negative feelings exert a negative influence on his inner mind. He rejects your application outright.

In daily life-activities you should not find yourself assailed by doubts and disputations. Express your ideas firmly and fearlessly. It is bound to exert a positive influence on the person. It also helps accomplish the job.

Whatever you think affects your *pran shakti.* Your negative thinking weakens this energy. The base and foundation of your personality is nothing but this *pran shakti.* It invests your voice with a particular kind of seriousness. It gives a brilliant glow in your eyes which affects your company. If you have a heightened *pran shakti,* others will feel totally subdued in your presence.

When you go to see your friend or any superior officer, a far better course would be that you look straight into his eyes. Put your ideas across with a certain measure of boldness and frankness. While talking do not try to look the other way round. You must talk without any diffidence. Do not keep saying—I mean—I mean. Do not feel overinclined to acknowledge mistakes. Do not have an apologetic tone. It reduces your *pran shakti.* With a weakened form of this energy you will be prone to dictates and domination. You will feel totally subdued. The talks will end up in utter failure.

With a view to strengthening your *pran shaki,* you must remain firm and determined. Advance with a postulate that you are right: Whatever you are saying is correct. The job with which you have gone to your superior officer will certainly be done. Your decision will prevail.

At the same time you are to be very careful when your boss or friend chooses to talk with you. While they are talking, do not look into their eyes. Or else you will go under their influence and your personality will seem to be weaker.

When you talk with somebody, do not look side ways. You must have your say with a firmness and you look straight into the eyes of the person you are talking with.

135

Stable Hypnotism

The persons who are employed are required to see their bosses several times. They are required to communicate what they feel like. They are also required to put up with what they have to say. At times serious differences crop up. In a situation like this, they must be firm and have their say with emphasis. If they choose to talk with the officers looking deeply into their eyes, they may take it that half of the job is as good as done. For they have in their eyes a magnetic power. It influences the person sitting opposite. In any case they must make sure that when they go to see their boss they must not suffer from any hesitation or diffidence. Neither should they have any inferiority complex.

To succeed in such confrontations, better they take to what is called *mirror tratak*. They must practise it regularly. They are to look deeply into the eyes of the reflection in the mirror. It will thus give them a good practice of *mirror tratak.*

In order to achieve success in life it is necessary that we are invested with hypnotic power. Your eyes will be particularly helpful. At the same time your style of conversation will also contribute to the making of your personality. Whenever you come across a friend of yours, do not start off with your own tale. If you do so you will lose your own attractiveness. On the contrary, provide him with the opportunity to talk as much as he wants. The less you talk, the greater will be your success.

In some persons we come across an undesirable habit. As soon as they meet they start telling us all about their petty troubles. A typical utterance in this situation is—I am sick. I am suffering from some malady. I may have cancer.

We give you an analogue. When the patient first went to the physician, the latter identified the disease. Later when he tested the patient which, in this case, was not at all warranted, he gave out jaundice as the cause of ailment. The results in either case were alike. Nonetheless the patient got a special kind of consolation. He would praise the physician. The physician, he says, made a thorough investigation. He heard him and confirmed that it was jaundice.

What I mean to say is that the prospective hypnotists should give a patient hearing to all people whether they talk sense or non-sense. They should seem to be enjoying the supply of information being made.

Suppose you come across a child. Why not fondle it? Suppose you come across a superbly attired bride. Why not praise her? Thus you are likely to win their hearts.

Woman is most vulnerable when it comes to her beauty. To activise your own wife it is at times necessary that you praise her. Tell her, for instance, that she looks shatteringly beautiful in this particular *saree*[1]. Why, she looks at least 10 years younger. She will certainly feel very happy.

Several situations one has to face in daily life. You come across your family members, your friends and your relations in a plurality of life situations almost daily. In order to sustain your attraction for them you have got to utter a word of praise for them. You must not overdo this job lest it should be taken as fooling business. If you give an impression of making false praise, your effort will be counterproductive.

Suppose you are going to see a friend of yours who is a patient in some nursing home. It should always be to your advantage if you carry with you a nice, beautiful present for him. It may be as little an object as a rose flower. Meeting him better you do not talk about his ailment at some length. No use giving him extra information about the ailment he is suffering from. A simple comment that he looks far better now will create the right atmosphere. Tell him you chanced to see a physician of his on your way to the nursing home. It was the physician who told you that the patient had almost recovered and would be discharged shortly.

Your words will make a soothing impact on the patient. Even after discharge he will not fail to thank you for the kind words. He will remain a most devoted friend throughout.

In order to progress in life you must have cultivated a strong memory. Suppose you are meeting a certain individual after a lapse of 5 years. If you could call him by his first name, you have almost won him over. On the contrary, if you fail to remember his name, you will lose whatever attraction you have for him.

Napoleon Bonaparte was the most famous general. One of the principal reasons of his fame was that he knew his soldiers— each one by his name. The very fact that such a distinguished general knew each soldier by his name was good enough for his soldiers. And, as a result, they were ever prepared to sacrifice everything to carry out the commands of such a general.

POINTS OF SUCCESS

The reader must have realised that we garner fresh experiences in every moment of our life. Every minute of our life we come across many persons. We give below certain points which ensure success in our private and public relations.

1. Always keep smiling. A happy and smiling face attracts many people. Nobody would like to keep company of sad and morose people.
2. Do not always recount your own personal problems. For this reason people will avoid you.
3. Praise the people who come to see you. You must, however, be balanced in your praise. They must not go away with the impression that they have been befooled.

---

1. *Saree:* A favourite apparel of Indian women.

4. Give more talking time to the other person. You yourself talk the least.
5. You must be dressed tastefully. Do not be shallow in the choice of words. Try to put your thoughts across in sober language.
6. When you see any high official or big person do not hesitate while talking with him. With all modesty and yet with a measure of firmness you place before them whatever you want to say.
7. You should not overdo the common courtesy of acknowledging your mistakes. Do not be too apologetic whether the situation warrants or not.
8. Do not allow yourself to be dominated by anger. If the person opposite is furious, prefer to keep cool. Later he will repent for having given vent to his anger. You will gain in respect and honour when you coolly put up with his anger.

Knowledge of Hypnotism

9. Whenever you see anybody particularly your friend, call him by his first name. The choice of your talking points should be such that he should find it very interesting and tasteful.

10. Mix up in a better society. If you move in a society of betters you will gain a lot. You will gain little if you keep yourself confined to people of your own rank.

11. Make acquaintance with people of high standards. If you are a physician, there is no use why you keep yourself confined only to physicians. You should have a wider spectrum of your company. Better you mix up with legal luminaries, high officials, prosperous businessmen, and senators. Your friendship with such diverse dignitaries will be in your own interest.

12. As far as possible do not tell lies or keep yourself to minimum if it cannot be helped. A lie does not survive for long.

13. Always keep yourself fresh. Nobody wants to mix with the sickly, the indolent and the exhausted. If you give others an impression of being dejected and frustrated, you will not be able to progress in life. Nor will you have a decent position in society.

14. Do not frequent low-class restaurants. Visit well-appointed and high class restaurants regardless of the frequency of your visits. For the company you will get at such choice places will be a choice company of bigger people. This company will do you good and improve your position in society. On the other hand, if you are found in cheap and low-class eating houses you will lose all respect in society.

15. You should not be given to eating on roads and streets. Better avoid company of such people who use undignified language while eating on roads and streets.

16. Your dress should be tasteful and neat and clean. It should reflect your temperament. Choice of dress should not be dictated by the prejudices of your company.

17. At least once or twice you must present gifts to your friends and highly placed officials. A gift is never little. But the gift

should be such that it can be preserved or made use of in decorating the drawing room.

18. Do not talk critically of any other friend while talking with a certain friend. Similarly you should not criticise any other official while talking with a certain official.

19. Keep your memory sharp and as far as possible keep remembering the names of your friends and relations.

20. Make it a point that your talks must lead to the sublimation of the ego of the person you are talking with.

21. Do not ask people to lend you anything. If somebody has borrowed money, of you, do not ask for refund. First do not lend, and suppose for some compelling reason you have lent him some money, do not give him notices for refund. On the other hand, if you have promised somebody to lend him money on a certain date, better pay him a couple of days before the scheduled date. It will help increase your position in society.

These are facts of the life of the hypnotist. Following these tips you will make yourself quite popular and acceptable in society.

12. SELF-HYPNOTISM

In the preceding pages we have already discussed all about a number of aspects concerning hypnotism. The base of hypnotism, we have seen, is the mind. It is through the mind that we can influence others. It is, therefore, all the more necessary that our mind is idea-free as far as possible. For the idea-free mind gives us greater strength and assumes a more effective capacity to influence others.

An idea-free mind is also the generating principle of *pran shaki*. Indeed this energy is very essential in our life, for it not only ensures total dissociation of ideas from the mind but also vests our face with a divine glow—a striking appearance which creates a profound and lasting impact on others. It also helps increase a special kind of magnetic power in our body. It, again, is highly important. For this power also gives an unusual brilliance to our eyes which is as helpful to influence others.

It is, therefore, very important that we preserve and strengthen this energy in our system.

In the preceding pages we have also discussed how we can gain control over the mind of the other person or how we can induce in him hypnotic sleep and how we can make him amenable to our purposes through hypnotic sleep. We have already discussed the various stages in hypnotism. One can always get success in the very first stage. In the third stage, however, one can accomplish perfect success. For instance, if the surgeon operates upon a hypnotised person, the latter will feel no pain whatsoever.

So far we have discussed the methods to hypnotise others. But it has a tremendous potential to accomplish self-hypnotism too. For one could confront and weaken and also eliminate many physical ailments and mental maladies through hypnotism. If at all we achieve the technique of self-hypnotism, we can as well cure ourselves of similar ailments and maladies and derive a lot of benefits.

The hypnotist can hypnotise others. Following the same principle he can hypnotise himself.

EXPERIMENTS OF SELF-HYPNOTISM

We describe below some experiments calculated to bring about self-hypnotism.

1. As far as possible make your mind idea-free. Try also to make your brain thought-free. When you have obtained this state of being you can set in the process of self-hypnotism.

   Early in the morning or evening practise *shirshasan*[1] for a few minutes. It will give you a lot of help to bring about an idea-free mind. After this stage, sit cool and collected on an *asana* for some time and fix your eye steadfastly in a certain direction. This part of the exercise will cool the sensual desires, if any, in you.

   After this stage try to rouse your inner mind, and suggest to your inner mind that you are getting sleepy, your eyes have gone very heavy and you are about to fall asleep soundly. Forestall at this stage all other thoughts seeking to rise in your mind. Fix your one-point concentration only on sleep.

   Gradually your inner mind will start receiving your suggestion. It will make you amenable to fall asleep. As a help to this process you better lie down actually. You may fall asleep while sitting. It will, however, not be a natural sleep. It will only be hypnotic sleep. You will lose yourself in this sleep. For you do not have any control over your inner mind at this stage. Make sure that as you are about to fall asleep, you will suggest to your inner mind that you must wake up in an hour all by yourself.

   Let there be no mistaking about the fact that you yourself will wake up all on your own in an hour.

---

1. *Shirshasan:* A *yogic* practice requiring the practitioner to stand on his head.

The hypnotic sleep will prove to be very soothing and sweet. You will seem as though you are floating on high waves and you are in motion in a charming world. You will be liberated from all kinds of mental tension and you will experience a special kind of delight.

Hypnotic State

2. In the evening or at night when you have gone through all activities of the day you lie down like a dead body, loosening all parts of the body.

   At this stage you suggest to your inner mind that a hypnotist is standing right in front of you and that he is trying to hypnotise you. In the same way you suggest to your inner mind that the hypnotist is asking you to go to sleep, and that as he informs so your eyes are getting pretty sleepy and you are prone to fall asleep. He also informs that you are going to have a sound sleep and that you will automatically wake up in an hour.

   You will see that the suggestion itself brings about sleep and that you wake up in an hour.

3. In the day time or at night you spread out an *asana* in any of your rooms and take seat on it with steadfastness. Try to concentrate your mind. After this stage try to suggest to yourself that you are feeling sleepy. The hypnotic sleep is getting better of you. Your eyes are already feeling very heavy. You are having a sound sleep.

144

If you regularly practise this exercise at a fixed time you will find that at the same time regularly you will start feeling sleepy. You will go to sleep automatically. This kind of sleep is very soothing and sweet.

4. At noon spread your *asana* and take seat comfortably. Place a mirror in front of you. You will see your face in bold outlines. When you see your face reflected in the mirror, you close your eyes. Try to advance your face. However you must make sure that your eyes remain fully closed. Remember you are seeing your face mentally.

The moment your face will go out of your mental sight you will start entering the realm of hypnotic sleep. Soon the hypnotic sleep will overtake you.

5. Cool and collected lie down on bed. Start chanting a mantra. Make sure that the mantra is not longish. You can, for instance, chant *Ram-Ram* or something as short as this. In the initial stage chant *Ram* a hundred times per minute. Now you slow down your speed. Gradually chant *Ram* twenty times a minute. This will increase the gap between one *Ram* and the subsequent *Ram.* Make sure that no other thought crosses your mind at this time.

As you will continue to slow down your speed, the time-gap between the two words will increase, which will certainly contribute to making your mind totally idea-free. The widening of the time-gap is very conducive to the dissociation of your mind from ideas.

It is during this process of dissociation that you will come under hypnotic spell. You will start feeling sleepy and in a few moments you fall asleep soundly.

6. Lie down on bed at night. Let diverse thoughts occupy your mind. If at all you find some of the many thoughts slipping away from your mind, you try to bring in more thoughts, making it a veritable crowd of thoughts.

After some time your mind and brain will feel totally tired because of the pressure of the ever-new thoughts assailing them. Being tired they will try to go to sleep. Your eyes, as a result, will feel rather heavy. The sleep you are put to at that time is nothing but hypnotic sleep.

This experiment has been very successful. It does not involve any great effort. If you try as suggested you will fall asleep in a few moments. When the mind gets cluttered up with a multiplicity of ideas, it begins to feel tired. The feeling of tiresomeness drives all ideas from the mind. The brain as also the mind is made fully devoid of all thoughts and ideas. As a result you fall asleep.

BENEFITS OF SELF-HYPNOTISM

One cannot but ask what are the benefits of self-hypnotism. Of course there are some benefits when we hypnotise others. For instance we can ask him a number of questions. We can ascertain the ideas which lie dormant in his mind. Could we achieve anything from self-hypnotism? When we hypnotise ourselves, who is there to ask questions and who is there to elicit answers?

There is an easy way out. When you hypnotise yourself you better tell your inner mind what all you want to know. This suggestion should be made shortly before you hypnotise yourself. At the same time you also suggest to the inner mind that you must remember the knowledge you have acquired even after you are restored to consciousness. When, after this stage, you get into hypnotic sleep, your inner mind takes care to remember your questions. When you wake up, you begin to remember the answers to your questions.

ADDITIONAL BENEFITS

Self-hypnotism ensures us many additional benefits:

1. It cures our mind of headache, inferiority complex, imaginary fears, etc.
2. When you are self-hypnotised, you obtain a strength in your thoughts. When the mind is made thought-free, it strengthens your memory. It helps you release from habits such as smoking and contributes to release from all bad habits.
3. It cures you of insomnia.

4. You gain in self-determination and it improves your will-power.
5. It secures your mind concentration.
6. Your ideas gain in creativity. This helps you gain a special strength and success in life.
7. It helps you release from all kinds of worries, and makes your life amenable to higher pursuits.
8. Through self-hypnotism you see yourself. You recognise yourself and you come to know your own weak points and what you are, in essence.

In short, self-hypnotism gives man a new self-confidence, which contributes to immense success in life.

13. POST-HYPNOTISM

In this chapter we shall examine post-hypnotism. By post-hypnotism we mean a study of the behaviour of the person after dehypnotisation. We have already shown that whatever suggestions are made to the person during his hypnotic state remain by and large stable. Post-hypnotism has made a penetrating study of such suggestions after the patient is restored to his normal consciousness and found that the suggestions remain stable even after dehypnotisation. To this extent this field makes a new enquiry and a separate subject.

A certain hypnotist brought a chain smoker under hypnotic influence and suggested that he finds the initial two puffs quite good. But as he takes the third puff he develops an aversion and feels compelled to throw away the cigarette.

After suggesting these ideas he brought him back to consciousness and began to talk with him on politics. For a couple of minutes the 'medium' exercised restraint. However, he felt a compelling urge to smoke. He brought out a cigarette and began to smoke. He found nothing wrong with the initial two puffers. But as he began to take the third puff, he found the whole thing pretty revolting. The taste it left in his mouth was so bitter that he wanted to throw away the cigarette at once. Eventually he threw it away. He, however, complained that these days the packing was being done rather carelessly. The standards of packing cigarettes had fallen very low.

He took out another. Taking the first two puffs he did not feel much of difference. But the third puff tasted so bitter that he had to throw it away. He thought as though he had consumed some foul matter.

At this stage the hypnotist offered to give him a different brand if he wanted to smoke. The 'medium' began to smoke that brand. The third puff gave him the same bitter taste. He threw it away. He said the weather had changed. Perhaps this was the reason why every cigarette tasted bitter.

The hypnotist said that he himself was smoking the same brand. He did not find it bitter. The 'medium' asked why he found it so bitter. Now he asked his servant to fetch a new packet. He smoked from this new packet and found it equally bitter.

He felt baffled. The hypnotist explained that he had post-hypnotised him (the 'medium') and that was the reason why he was finding all cigarettes bitter.

The hypnotist, once again, post-hypnotised him and suggested that he would no longer find the cigarette bitter and that he would relish smoking as before. At this he terminated the post-hypnotic state.

The 'medium' smoked and relished smoking. There was nothing bitter about the cigarette.

What it implies is that post-hypnotism by itself is a very effective medium. We can make a person renounce his bad habits through the instrumentality of post-hypnotism. Thus we can help him live a healthy and balanced life.

In the West the vogue of post-hypnotism has a more extensive acceptability. Its use on patients, particularly, is said to be very effective. Generally patients being brought under post-hypnotism are told how they are to conduct themselves in the absence of the physician and which medicine they are to take at such and such hours and how the medicines are to be administered.

In the absence of the physician the patient follows the directions which the physician had given him through post-hypnotism. The physician finds it particularly helpful in curing the patient of his diseases.

Once a gentleman came to me from Aligarh. He complained that his daughter fell in love with a youth. The youth belonged to a lower caste. If at all they marry the family would earn a bad name. He had persuaded her to call off the step, but she did not seem to be willing. The girl, too, had come along with him.

I talked with the girl. She seemed to be very firm in her ideas and language. She said she accepted the youth as her husband. She cared a fig for what he was and to which caste he belonged. It made no difference to her. She was in no position to give him up.

Right in the presence of her father I suggested to the girl through post-hypnotism that the boy she loved was of a loose character. In fact he made a show of love. He would give her up the moment he achieved his personal end. He would make her miserable. It would be in her interest to give him up. When she would be restored to her consciousness she would develop a burning hatred for the youth. The love would vanish.

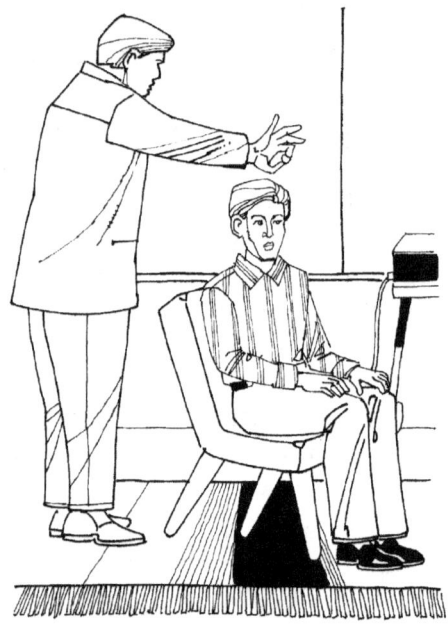

Hypnotism

Soon after I terminated her hypnotism. However I did not tell her anything. Both father and daughter left for Aligarh by the noon train. Within fifteen days I got a letter from the gentleman of Aligarh. The girl had a big fight with the boy. Now she hated him intensely. She got furious when the very name of the boy was referred to. The love was over.

In a few days the gentleman got her married to a deserving youth. Both lived happily.

What I mean to say is that with the help of this technique we can always fight socially subversive tendencies and ensure that the society remains stable.

A similar experiment was once conducted by a certain person at the Hypnotism Conference at Ahmedabad. He selected a member of the audience and brought him under post-hypnotic spell. He suggested that he would wake him up and then address the Conference for a full hour. While addressing the Conference he would place his finger on the table, and as he would do so, the 'medium' would start scratching his head with both hands. It was at this stage, he said, he would terminate the spell.

As he suggested the hypnotist while addressing the Conference placed his finger on the table. The same moment the 'medium' began to scratch his head, while other members of the audience did not feel any itching sensation. It was noticed that the hypnotist during his address must have placed his finger on the table twenty times and each time the 'medium' scratched his head, while the other members of the audience remained wholly unaffected.

It is now very clear from this experiment that only the 'suggested' person comes under hypnotic influence, and none else. The other important point is that the suggestion implanted through post-hypnotism remains quite stable until it is withdrawn duly.

The third point is that the same hypnotist can withdraw the suggestion, and no other hypnotist.

After the address was over, the hypnotist of the Ahmedabad Conference brought the same 'medium' under post-hypnotic spell and suggested that in future anybody touching the table with his finger, he would not scratch his head. Now would he entertain any idea like this?

Later the same hypnotist spoke on couple of occasions to the same audience, and the said person did not feel compelled to scratch his head.

A hypnotist, to take another practice, suggests to a person whom he has already taken under his post-hypnotic spell that he will fall asleep as soon as he (the hypnotist) snaps his finger thrice. Similarly he implants the same suggestion to another person. In the same way, at different times, he implants the same suggestion to fifteen persons separately at different times. Suppose chance brings all these different people at one place at one time. As soon as the hypnotist snaps his finger thrice, the fifteen of them will at once fall asleep. It is not at all necessary to snap fingers separately for each one of them.

In the foregoing lines I have emphasised that the 'medium' sitting opposite will carry out the suggestion as made. At the same time one can implant suggestions in a person or persons living thousands of miles away.

To illustrate this point, suppose you suggest to a person living a thousand miles away that when he received your letter he would be remembering only you for all his 24 hours. During these 24 hours he would not relish even eating and drinking.

Self-Hypnotism

After this, whenever your letter reaches him, he would go crazy for the subsequent 24 hours.

The point I want to make is that one can have anything done by suggesting and working up post-hypnotic trance by post.

In foreign countries, and not in India, the vogue of putting up successful public performances of hypnotism has already picked up. One finds the organisers are making good money out of these performances. Hypnotism, basically, is a science, and so if somebody is seeking to make money out of this science there is nothing objectionable about it. But in any case it must be ensured that nobody is cheated and nobody is allowed to get away with only personal gains.

We give below some points about hypnotic performances. We hope readers can make use of these points to sort out the problems of livelihood.

1. First of all your personality should be very impressive. You should dress yourself tastefully and it should conform to the needs of the changing weather. You must remember that it is only an impressive personality which makes on the audience a profound and lasting impact.

   When you appear on the stage to give a public performance, you should not take more than 5 to 7 minutes to tell the audience all about hypnotism and particularly how soon it creates its impact. You must also add that it is nature which has provided in each individual the potential to be drawn under hypnotic spell. So the entire audience sitting in front of you can be brought under hypnotic influence.

   This short introduction will contribute to setting the right tone. The audience will begin to feel that they can be influenced. For God created us with this potential.

   Now, at this stage, in a serious and sober tone you tell the audience that you are seeing all of them. Better they look at you. They look into your eyes. You are looking into the eyes of each one of them and you are evaluating in a most effective way each one of them.

   Soon after, you place firmly both your hands on the table. Now fix your eye on the entire audience and try to look into the eyes of each member. It will give you their

153

attention. They will feel compelled to look into your eyes. The looks will collide. They themselves will fall to hypnotic trance.

Now, in a firm and forthright tone, ask the audience to interlock their fingers (of hands). When the audience have done so, tell them that their fingers got stuck up in interlocked relations and even if they try to disengage them, it will not be possible to do so.

In a vibrant tone ask them to have a try and tell them howsoever they might try they will not be able to disengage their interlocked fingers.

During this exercise you will be able to spot out who of them could prove to be an amenable 'subject' for you. For the individuals who would not be able to set apart their hands even after repeated attempts will prove to be excellent 'subjects' for you.

Now you summon 15 to 20 of such 'subjects' to the rostrum. Ask them to be seated in chairs provided on the stage. After

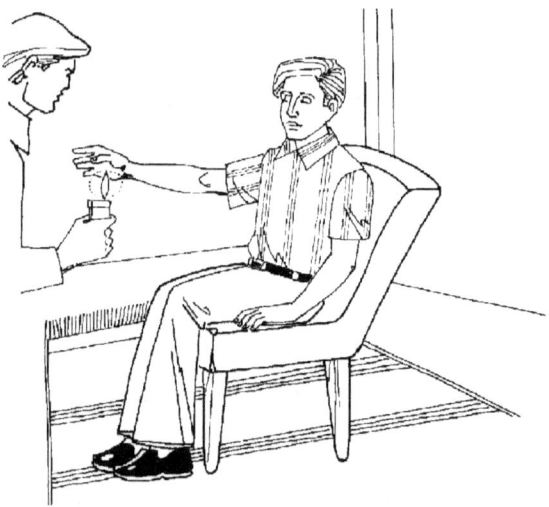

The Hand does not burn during Hypnotic Spell

they take seats, tell them that you have separated their hands. Now they would not face any difficulty in separating their hands. They can disengage their hands.

The moment you say so, the interlocked fingers of these individuals will come out of the knot. They will heave a sigh of relief. Now ask them to resume their allotted seats.

The persons who are on the stage will prove to be better assistants in your experiments. For they are more amenable 'subjects'. The people who are seated in the auditorium are simply audience who will merely see your experiments

Ask each of your 'subjects' to sit separately. Tell all of them that they are under your hypnotic spell and that they are bound to carry out whatever you ask them to do.

At this stage you fix your attention to your 'subjects'. Tell them that they are already tired being seated for long. They want to drop asleep in the chairs. Their eyes are getting very heavy.

Ask them to sleep. Let them close their eyes. They are feeling sleepy. They have fallen asleep. Let them rest their heads against the back of the chair.

The spectators will feel amazed that the subjects have fallen asleep as soon as you have suggested. They are sleeping soundly. Some of them are snoring as well.

Now select a 'subject' and give him paper and a pen. Tell him to write on the paper what you are dictating. Ask him to hold the pen. Tell him to pick up the paper from the left side. Ask him to write whatever you say.

"I am useless. I am like garbage. So I should be picked up and dumped in a bin."

Ask him to append his signature to this statement. Let him mention the date and ask him to write down his address.

You will see that he has written exactly in the same manner as you have suggested.

Now terminate his hypnotic sleep. There are others who are still sleeping hypnotically. Suggest to these persons that as you snap your fingers thrice, they will wake up. Also suggest that they will not remember what you have told them during their hypnotic sleep.

Now snap your fingers thrice. They will all wake up from

155

hypnotic sleep as soon as they hear your fingers snapping.

Ask the 'subject' who took down on paper whatever you dictated to tell you his name.

He will quote his name. Ask him what post he is holding. He will describe his post, which must seem to be rather very important. Ask him whether his department needs his services or he is useless in the department.

It is natural he will assert that he is a very important officer and that he is quite capable of administering the department. He will add that the State or Central Govern-ments have so far received no complaints against him.

Now you turn your attention to the audience. Tell the audience that this gentleman says that he is a very important person and a capable officer.

At this stage turn your attention to your 'subject' and inform him that he has already written to the Government that he is a useless person and so he is no better than garbage.

He will certainly protest that being a responsible officer he would not write anything like that.

You hand over the note to him. He will be shocked to see his own statement in his own handwriting, duly signed.

Ask him whether he should be dumped in the bin. He will certainly feel quite nonplussed. As he will be losing colours in his face, the audience will feel totally surprised.

Tear the paper into pieces in front of him and tell him that it was obtained through hypnotism. Assure him that he is quite a capable and responsible officer. With this request ask him to take his seat.

The audience will find the whole exercise rather incredible and pleasantly surprising.

2. Select a 'medium' and ask him to appear on the stage, and stand facing the audience. It would be better if a female offers herself to be 'medium' for this practice. A male, too, can make do in this situation.

Ask her to keep standing on the stage. You yourself take a standing position exactly behind her, and hold your both hands parallelly rather close to her ears.

At this stage you suggest to her that as you would draw your hands back, she would also feel being drawn back. Or she might feel as though some power is pushing her behind and causing her to fall. You assure that she need not worry. You are standing behind and you will hold her in any case.

As you have said so, start drawing your hands back. You will see that the 'medium', too, will start getting drawn to her back.

Now you suggest to her that she is falling behind. She is falling precipitately. Tell her that you are standing behind and that you have kept your hands outstretched. You are holding her and that she is resting on your arms.

You will see that as you go on suggesting to her, the 'medium' would be receding back, almost falling to her knees and so she would be resting on your arms.

This experiment will almost electrify the audience and your name and fame would spread far and wide in the world of hypnotism.

3. Make the 'subject' seated on the other end of the table. Ask him to rest his hand on the table. Make sure that the portion of the hand—from elbow to the finger—should rest on the table and the palm too. Now suggest that his hand is resting on the table and it (the hand) has gone heavier than necessary. Tell him that the hand is feeling so heavy that he will not be able to lift it up despite attempts.

Ask him to lift his hand up from the table. You will notice that he will not be able to do so, although he has tried his best. He is clearly upset. But he fails to raise his hand despite all efforts.

Turn your attention to the audience and tell them that you have made his hand resting on the table so heavy that he will not be able to raise it up in spite of efforts.

Give another opportunity to the 'subject' to exert all force and raise his hand from the table. But he fails, although he has put in serious efforts. He feels terribly put out.

At this stage suggest that you are making his hand light so that he can raise it above the table and reach his normal state of being. Tell him that you have already made the hand light. He can now raise it above the table. His hand is back to normal.

Hypnotic State of Being

Finally suggest to him to raise his hand from the table. Now he raises his hand without any effort, and he seems fully satisfied.

4. Call a 'subject' to the stage and ask him to stand in front of you. Put a coin (of any value) in his right palm. Take care that you have already shown the coin to the audience so that they know it is a common coin and that it does not have any speciality about it.

Having put the coin in his palm ask him to look into your eyes. When he does so, suggest that the coin which he is holding is unique and that it is vested with some special qualities.

Suggest to him: The coin is hotting up. Slowly it has gone red-hot. It is burning your palm. The coin has gone red. The skin of your palm has been burnt out. You are feeling a terrible pain. The coin has gone so hot that you can no longer hold it in your palm.

Following your suggestion the 'subject' will start feeling that his palm is actually burning and his skin too. Terribly confused, he will fling the coin away as though it is actually ablaze.

The audience will feel terribly fascinated.

5. Bring a 'subject' on to the stage. Make him stand in front of you. Ask him to try to look into your eyes. However, take care that you do not look into his eyes, for often it involves loss to the hypnotist himself. The implication is that if the 'subject' himself is a hypnotist or if he has more magnetic power, you yourself will fall to his hypnotic power, not the 'subject'. So you should exercise utmost caution in this matter.

When you will find him looking into your eyes, tell him that he is feeling weak in himself and so he has been trying to sit down. Also tell him that his legs are not lending themselves to bend. He is unable even to keep standing. He is falling behind. He has already bent very low to the back. Now he is actually falling behind.

You notice that he is actually falling behind. You rush to him and give him support in your arms.

This experiment will impress the audience tremendously.

6. Choose from the audience a 'subject' and have him on the stage. Make sure that he is a good 'subject'. Over a protracted experience one does come to know how one can lend himself to be a good 'subject'. To test who can be a good 'subject', put the audience to one or two simple tests. You will know who amongst the audience is a good 'subject'. Choose one amongst them and have him on the stage. In any case, take care that he is not a high official or leader.

Ask him to sit in a chair on the stage. Make sure that he faces the audience. Look into his eyes and hypnotise him. When he is fully hypnotised suggest that he has come under your total control and so whatever you would suggest, he would act upon it without questioning. Also tell him that whenever you would snap your fingers he will bark like a dog.

Now terminate the hypnotic state. Indeed he will seem to be a very normal person, but he will remember nothing. Let him sit in the chair in the same way.

Now you spend some time with the audience. Engage them in some interesting talks. Make sure that you have whiled away five minutes.

Next you snap your fingers. The moment you do so, the 'subject' will start barking like a dog.

The audience will find the whole thing amazing. Coming across a dog's barking they will drown themselves into interminable laughter. When, at least, the 'subject' ceases to bark, you, once again, snap your fingers. It will set him barking again.

Now you, once again, hypnotise the 'subject' and cause him to sleep hypnotically. During this state of being, suggest to him that he has been freed from this effect. Tell him that he will not bark like a dog when you snap your fingers.

Terminate his hypnotism. Now deliberately snap your fingers in front of him. He will not bark, let alone do anything else. Send him back to the audience.

This performance will drive home that you are an outstanding hypnotist and your reputation will reach far and wide.

7. Select a 'subject' from the audience and have him on the stage. Make sure that the 'subject' is well-built and very strong physically. Make him stand in front of you and hypnotise him. When he has been put to hypnotic sleep suggest that he is very strong and that his physique is very healthy and rugged. Also tell him that his body has gone very stiff. It has gone still and cold. He is no longer in a position to keep standing. So you are making him lie. He has his feet on a chair and head on another. There is nothing to bridge the gap between the two chairs. Since he is very stiff he could lie down on the two chairs

like a stiff wooden log. Make him lie down. Ensure that you have put nothing to bridge the gap between the two chairs.

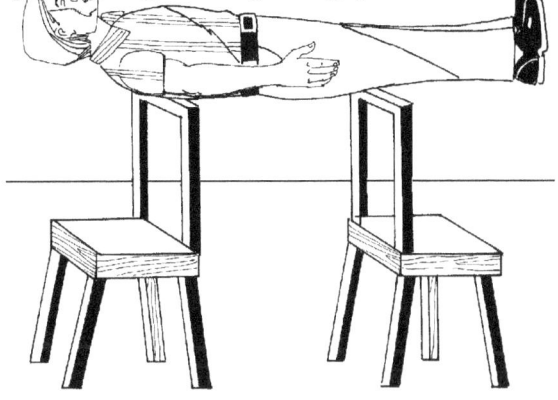

Hypnotic

Suggest that his body is stiff like a wooden log. If you or anybody else stands on his stiff body, his body despite the pressure will not bend. He will continue to lie on the two chairs like a wooden log. Neither will it cause any pain to him.

Get on to his chest and keep standing. You find he remains unchanged like a strong wooden log. He does nothing to suggest that he is being put to the uses of wooden logs.

For a minute or two keep standing on his chest. Come away slowly. The audience will feel thrilled to see these incredible feats.

Now suggest that he is fast being restored to his normal state. Now he is in a position to keep standing. You are making him stand up.

You help him stand up and suggest that his body has been restored to its flexible character. The body has all actions going on within. His eyes are getting open. He is now awake. His eyes have actually opened.

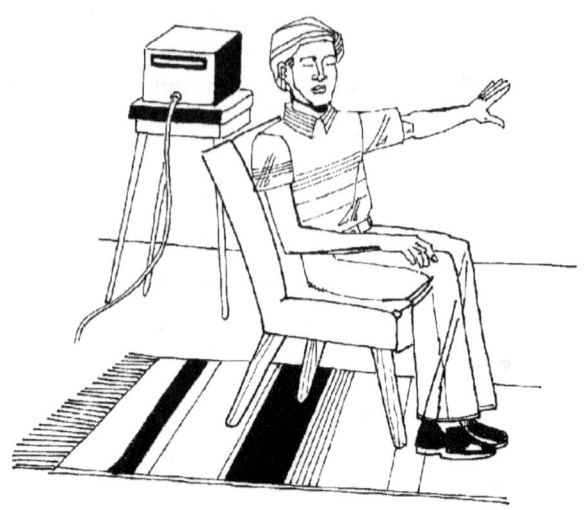

Hypnosis

You will notice that the 'subject' has woken up and that his body has become flexible once again.

The audience will be greatly influenced by this feat. In any case, make sure that the 'subject' is not a weakling.

8. When you are putting up a public performance, it is essential that it should make an effective and desirable impact on the audience. You could take to a certain method.

In a serious and sonorous voice you tell the audience that the science of hypnotism is extraordinarily effective, and every member of the audience could be brought under the impact of hypnotism.

Tell them that you will no longer look into their eyes. You will rather get behind the screen and seek to hypnotise the audience from behind the screen. Tell them that you are quite sure that as a result of your efforts the audience will feel sleepy and eventually they will go to sleep.

Now, finally, you give a deep and penetrating gaze at your audience, and get behind the screen.

From behind the screen you proclaim: Now all of you are under my control and under hypnotic influence. You seem to be tired. You want to sleep. Now rest your head against the back of the chair and go to sleep. You have already got sleepy. Your eyes have gone very heavy. Your eyes are already closed. You are already asleep. When I clap thrice you will be able to wake up.

Come back to the stage. You will find that most of the members of the audience are already asleep in their chairs. Surely there would be some persons who keep awake. It means that they can never be good 'subject'. They, too, will feel bewildered to see so many people asleep.

Now clap thrice. Wake up all people. Suggest that they have got over their sleep. They are all hale and hearty, besides being quite normal.

9. Call upon the stage a successful 'subject' and hypnotise him. Suggest that he is in sound sleep and that you are making him lie down on this large table. Also suggest that he has got to such sound sleep that he will not be able to open his eyes nor wake up, howsoever one may shout into his ears.

   Make the 'subject' lie down on the table within the full view of the audience. Now call 2 or 3 persons from the audience and ask them to shout or clap or play on a horn to wake him up.

   These members of the audience will naturally shout at their loudest or blow a trumpet, but the 'subject' will not open his eyes. Nor will he wake up.

   The audience will feel simply dazed, for they know even a stone-deaf person would wake up, given the loud shoutings he has been subjected to.

   Now suggest to the 'subject' that he is in a position to wake up and he will wake up as soon as you snap your fingers.

   Snap your fingers once. The 'subject' will at once wake up. He will feel surprised to find the audience laughing.

The experiments described above can be successfully performed. You will develop a high measure of self-confidence. You will also know how capable you are in hypnotising others.

It will get you honour and respect, which will also contribute to making you an outstanding hypnotist.

In the following pages I am going to discuss how hypnotism will prove beneficial in the humdrum daily activities and how the whole thing could be made amenable.

OO

14. ADVANTAGES OF HYPNOTISM

The world today is more difficult and complex than ever. Life today is vitiated by unsuspect problems. The entire pattern has gone so vicious and so bafflingly complex.

There has been no remedy. In most cases the cure has proved more fatal than the disease. The more we are exposed to the helplessness of man poised against such unprecedented dangers to life and values, the better we see that a beginning must be made with the psyche. For the root of these infinite complexities has been the mental malady which resulted in all kinds of holocausts.

It is, therefore, imperative that we focus attention on the individual and on his mind. The individual's mind should be liberated from deepening tension, escalating fears, increasing panic and other intractable problems. It alone will give a different orientation to the mind. It alone has the potential to make the mind creative and constructive.

Hypnotism has a special role to play in the modern age. Generally people are agreed on its incomparable utility. It has, therefore, been accepted as a special and influential science in modern times. More than any other science, hypnotism focuses attention on the individual and on the mind.

There are many other problems in modern life. We can sort out these complex problems largely with the help of hypnotism.

In the preceding pages we have discussed how it helps in daily life situations too.

CURATIVE PROPERTIES

Hypnotism has been most significant in the field of curative properties. In modern times there are many ailments which do not respond to any medicines. The maladies of the mental patient, for instance, cannot be lessened or removed through the instrumentality of drugs and medicines.

It is only hypnotism which has a proven promise to tackle such incurable diseases. Man today is prone to run more risks than ever.

No wonder he has also become more vulnerable to mental worries and tension. One can hope to confront and eliminate these mental worries and tension only when one goes into the root causes which give rise to worries and tensions. It is certain that unless anxiety and worries are removed from his mind, he cannot be freed from these maladies. Anxiety is often said to have eaten into the vitals of man.

Hypnotism gives us hypnotic sleep, which liberates man from anxiety. He could be suggested that it is no use why he should continue to remain bogged down in the labyrinth of anxieties. The loss or the death is now an object of one's past. It is no use why we should continue to ponder over what is no more a matter of present concerns.

He could also be suggested that he would no longer remember the event which caused him anguish.

When he is restored to his consciousness he forgets clean the tragic event which has caused him untold misery and anguish. He comes to live a healthy and cheerful life.

If he continues to suffer from any special kind of mental malady or mental anguish, his mind could be made thought-free and idea-free. This will certainly restore him to a life of no anxiety and no anguish.

A certain person who had lost his young son once came to see me. He was deeply attached to his son. He literally became half-demented. He lost all interest in work. He would not even eat. Six months had passed. His family felt totally upset. For he was the only earning member in the family. He had stopped going to work. Now the family had no other source of livelihood. The family obviously fell on evil days.

The dead son used to haunt him day and night. He would never get over the son's abiding memory. It ate into the vitals of the man. He was reduced to a rickety frame. Emanciated and physically weak he was a shipreck of his old self.

When he came to me I noticed he conducted himself like a lunatic. Every moment, he, I noticed, felt haunted by his son's memory.

I made him sit in a chair and brought him under hypnotic influence. I suggested that nobody is father and nobody is son. All were, in fact, intertwined with individual interests.

Further I told him that he must account for his previous life. Surely he must have been indebted to the person who arrived in his family in the form of his son. Once the accounts were cleared, he preferred to withdraw from his obligations. Viewed from a spiritual angle, the deceased was not at all related to him. His exit was natural. Further I told him that he had no business to mourn the loss. It would rather cause the departed soul much pain.

Then I suggested that I would wake him up from hypnotic sleep. He would forget all about the deceased. He would pay all attention to his family. He would resume going to work. He would live his life successfully.

I suggested to him that he had forgotten his son wholly. He would not remember him even if somebody tried to remind him of his son.

Then, I terminated his hypnotic spell. He looked a normal person. He began to talk about his family with good cheer. For half an hour, I talked with him on all kinds of topics—society, politics and household. I saw him off.

Separately, I had instructed his wife to remove all belongings of her deceased son such as photos, dress, clothes etc. from the house.

The man has since been living a normal life. He no more remembers his son. He has been living his life cheerfully. Thus a family which had disintegrated was joined together and has since lived a life without worries and tension.

In this manner we can always liberate the individual from the impact of the tragic event which caused him anxiety and tension.

Hypnotism has evolved the vogue of painless surgical operations. Any limb can be operated upon with the help of hypnotism.

While sleeping hypnotically the patient is exposed to no pain or suffering. No longer do such patients need any morphia for this purpose.

∞

15. BLESSINGS OF HYPNOTISM

ROLE OF HYPNOTISM IN DELIVERY

In the West the vogue of hypnotism in delivery is very common place. It is largely due to the science of hypnotism that delivery nowadays is a painless affair. It does not need any operation either. Again, the delivery under hypnotic spell does not lead to any complications or harmful effects. It does not leave any adverse effects either on the person concerned.

ROLE OF HYPNOTISM IN DENTISTRY

In the US and other countries hypnotism is being increasingly used for the cure of a number of ailments. Teeth are extracted with the help of hypnotism. Now there is no need for local morphia.

Many other physical ailments such as pain, headache and stomach disorder, etc. are also being taken care of with the help of hypnotism.

This science has registered such a spectacular progress that it is no more necessary for the hypnotist to keep standing in front of his patient. Patients are being cured of their chronic diseases over telephone through long distance calls.

In Canada and other countries the doctor speaks to the expecting mother over phone: This is Dr..... I will count one, two and three. You will fall asleep. You will be able to negotiate your delivery without any pain or troubles. I see you are getting sleepy. Okay. Go to sleep. Go to sleep. Go to sleep.

This suggestion makes an immediate impact on the patient. The delivery she has during hypnotic sleep leaves her normal and comfortable.

EXPERIMENTS ON MENTAL PATIENTS

Hypnotism has been most effective in the field of mental diseases. It is essential that mental patients are told about hypnotism and explained how hypnotism contributes to the elimination of mental maladies.

The entire focus of hypnotism fails on the mind and the brain. It is, therefore, very natural that many ailments are eliminated since it makes a direct impact on the brain.

Doctors in the West hold that over 95 per cent patients who suffered from mental maladies have recovered with the help of hypnotism. And it needs no drugs and no medicines. No electric shocks either.

AMNESIA

As a result of injury on the head or fall from above, one loses one's memory. At times such a person forgets his name, address. etc. It causes undue problems to the doctors. Medical science does not know of any treatment or drug which brings to life the lapsed memory and cures the patient of amnesia or loss of memory.

However, hypnotism has found a way out. Through the medium of hypnotism the outer mind of the person is awakened. It is the outer mind which forgets the incidents of the past. But the inner mind being always active keeps a track record of all past happenings.

In a situation like this the hypnotist takes the patient into his confidence and puts him to hypnotic sleep. He awakens his inner mind and causes it to remember his past incidents. As a result it recounts the past incidents as it is. Then the person concerned is suggested that he will continue to remember all past incidents even after he is restored to consciousness. He will not be able to forget the past happenings even if he tries to do so.

After this stage the hypnosis is terminated. After being restored to consciousness he remembers with exactitude the events which he had forgotten as a result of head injury or fall.

One event leads to another. The events are interrelated. Thus he remembers all events of the past.

ROLE OF HYPNOTISM IN EDUCATION

Many of our readers may feel slightly surprised to know that in the West which puts a premium on science they are increasingly making use of hypnotism for education. They teach with the aid of hypnotism. Hypnotism helps students comprehend many difficult topics.

A certain student, for instance, has a tremendous aversion for physics and so he finds this subject unnecessarily difficult. To ensure that the student must cultivate the right approach for physics, the hypnotist puts him to hypnotic sleep. During this sleep the student is exposed to the difficult questions and answers of physics. He is suggested to retain in his memory what has already been explained. He is told that he will never forget the explanation.

He is suggested that physics in itself is a simple and fascinating subject. When he gets up, he remembers all these questions and answers and that his aversion will go.

Not only physics, all other subjects are taught during hypnotic sleep so that the student remains no more weak in any subject.

In so many countries a number of subjects are taught by way of records or cassettes. All hypnotists are not expected to be masters of all subjects. So answers to questions are taped or recorded.

At this stage the student is suggested that he will retain in memory whatever he has been told. Particularly after he regains his consciousness. Records or cassettes are then played giving lessons or topics which have a direct bearing on textual learning. The inner mind of the 'subject' receives the contents and when he wakes up, he remembers his lessons as it is.

It is often resorted to for defence and security purposes. Military experts hold that the lessons driven home in hypnotic sleep remain somewhat stable and one could provide a huge chunk of the prescribed learning in the shortest possible time. They argue that a course of studies designed to be imparted for a period of one year can as well be crammed in a mere three months' time taking advantage of the hypnotic technique. They disclosed that the soldiers poised to fight the Chinese were equipped with the knowledge of warfare in the short period of only three months. Normally it takes one full year to impart the same teaching.

The news item published in *Los Angeles Express* dated October 24, 1949 further confirms this opinion.

During the War educationists began to see that it was easier to impart lessons through the inner mind rather than of the outer mind. Making use of the hypnotic techniques an array could be equipped in only three months to subdue the largest army of the world.

The famous American military expert Dr. Walker affirms that the outer mind forms only one-ninth of the entire mind. And yet it is this small part which has to take on the entire thrust of education. Instead of education is imparted to the inner mind the latter can absorb with far better ease and that there will be no obstacle standing in the way.

Dr. Walker further demonstrated that with the aid of hypnotism we could learn a new language in the best possible manner within the shortest possible time. Language teaching confined only to the outer mind has often proved to be an exercise in frustration.

Teaching of foreign languages to the armed forces in many foreign countries has been perfected using largely the technique of hypnotism. The learners are put to hypnotic sleep and records and cassettes containing well-graded lessons are played close to their ears. The inner mind takes hold of these lessons with no effort at all.

There is a tremendous pressure on time in the modern world. So we can achieve a good number of impossible tasks without much effort if we make proper use of hypnotic techniques. In education it has proved to be a boon.

SURGICAL OPERATIONS

Hypnotism is being increasingly used as an effective substitute for anaesthesia in operation theatres[1]. Now largely with the aid of hypnotism the patient can be put to hypnotic sleep without making use of anaesthesia. Even the need to go in for local anaesthesia in respect of certain limbs has been rendered unnecessary by hypnotism.

IMPACT ON TUBERCULOSIS

The disease takes an upper hand over us only when we lose our own in-built resistance. At the same time when a certain patient remains sick for some time and meanwhile does not gain control over his sickness, he loses his self-confidence.

Now, it is very easy to strengthen his self-confidence with the help of hypnotism. He can also be given resistance to fight the disease. Several Indian hypnotists conducted experiments on patients suffering from tuberculosis. However, the patients continued to take the prescribed medicines. They were surprised to see that the patient given hypnotic treatment recovered fully within a short period.

Normally, the patient takes one full year to overcome this disease. Hypnotism, however, restores him to full health within 4 to 6 months.

ROLE IN SKIN DISEASES

Medical experts hold that skin diseases are caused mainly due to the mental fears of the individuals. Although there are many factors leading to skin diseases, it is the mental state which principally accounts for this disease. When he finds a small insignificant part of his body developing this disease, he gets terribly scared. The scare itself leads to its escalation all over the body.

Hypnotists have found a way out. They put such patients to hypnotic sleep and suggest that he does not suffer very much from skin disease and that he will fully recover on the strength of a certain medicine. He will further suggest that the disease will not further spread out and he need not worry about.

It is certain that after the termination of the hypnotic sleep the patient will get over his anxiety and will mentally feel quite strong.

---

1. According to medical scientists anaesthesia weakens the heart. Often such patients, having been anaesthetised for heart operations, succumb during operation to death due to pressure of anaesthesia.

Thus hypnotism contributes a lot to the elimination of skin disease.

IMPACT ON ABDOMINAL TROUBLES

It is a truism that abdominal diseases stem from mental tension and anguish. Over 80% of such patients got their trouble due to mental anxiety. The people who keep on worrying about the advancement of their commerce and business are also the worst patients suffering from abdominal diseases.

Hypnotism has proved to be very effective in eradicating abdominal diseases. For hypnotism gives his mind a certain strength and through hypnosis he could be suggested that it is no use why he should continue to worry about. He is scared of a certain anxiety, but it will not trouble him in any way.

Further he could be suggested that he is not actually suffering from any abdominal disease. Nor does he have constipation or any of other troubles. He could be told that he will feel healthier and free from mental stress and strain when he wakes up.

ROLE IN ERADICATING PAINS AND ACHES

A good number of body pains and aches can be eradicated with the help of hypnotism Often we come across patients crying and writhing out of stomach pain. The patient does not get any relief, although he has had all kinds of medicines.

Treatment of any stubborn body pain and ache is now possible through hypnotism. The hypnotist puts the patient to hypnotic sleep and suggests that he is totally healthy, he has no trouble whatsoever and when he wakes up from hypnotic sleep he will certainly forget all about his pain.

Soon the hypnotic sleep is terminated. When he wakes up, he does not experience any restlessness or scare. He comes to feel very healthy.

Many similar experiments have been conducted in foreign countries. They have devised a good number of latest techniques to give a real relief to the patients. In India the vogue of such treatment is somewhat limited. But in other countries hypnotism is being increasingly resorted to for such purposes and also in all fields of medical treatment.

ROLE IN MAKING IDEAS FIRM

In modern times what is important is that one can succeed only when one is very firm in thoughts and when one is endowed with a rich, resonant personality.

One can have both these accomplishments through the medium of hypnotism. One of the postulates of hypnotism is that it can operate only when the human body has a certain degree of magnetic power. If it helps strengthen the magnetic power inherent in your body, your personality must emerge as very impressive and glorious. Indeed hypnotism is known to be the rock bottom of personality.

Besides, when we succeed in influencing others through the medium of hypnotism, we gain in our self-confidence.

It makes our thoughts firm, determined and mature which again make an extensive impact on our own life-pattern and we advance briskly from one success to another.

ROLE IN STRENGTHENING MEMORY

In the preceding lines we have already discussed that we can strengthen and develop our memory with the help of hypnotism. It is only when the brain does not entertain any irrelevant thoughts that we can hope to strengthen and develop our memory.

For the brain has a certain capacity, if irrelevant thoughts crowd in the brain the relevant thoughts will be crowded out.

We have already discussed the idea of the thought-free mind in some length. We have also seen how we can make our mind thought-free. The principal benefit of this experiment is that we can from now on preserve in our mind only such thoughts as we want to preserve. It is obvious once we do so, the irrelevant thoughts will have no room in the mind.

By obtaining, thus, a thought-free mind we can entertain only likeable and amenable thoughts. It will strengthen and develop our memory.

ROLE IN CONCENTRATION

One cannot have integrity in life if one cannot have an enriched concentration. For it is by concentration we develop insights in our fields and we can explore them in some depth.

Scholars hold that given a concentrated study of a subject or field one can achieve a complete success in a shorter period.

The mind goes stray. If we control the anarchical movements of the mind we can obtain concentration. As a result both mind and brain can achieve concentration on a certain point and achieve success in it.

Indeed concentration of the psyche has been the greatest accomplishment of man. In the Indian Yoga philosophy it is said that the person who has gained firm control over his stray thoughts can reach *Brahma*[1].

It is through hypnotism that we can achieve concentration of the mind. It gives us integrity in every walk of life.

ROLE IN CONTROLLING BODY TEMPERATURE

A certain degree of temperature is a must for the human being. If it slides below or goes beyond the optimum degree, he is taken ill. In order to maintain health and strength it is necessary that the body temperature remains stable.

In hypnotic state we can increase or decrease the temperature of the 'subject'. If somebody is running high temperature, he could be hypnotised and suggested that his temperature is far less than it was before and he has the optimum temperature.

After experiments it has been ascertained that the body temperature could be controlled through hypnotism. When the 'subject' wakes up, he finds himself free from his fever which caused interminal troubles.

Similarly it has been found to be highly useful in regulating blood pressure too.

It has proved very successful in all such troubles which owe their rise to fluctuations in body temperature.

---

1. *Brahma:* The Absolute Being.

ROLE IN MAKING DIVINE VISION

The human being has in his body innumerable ganglions which remain active and also control the working of the body. It is these ganglions which have made the human being distinct from animals. But over a long period man has overlooked the use of some ganglions. He has thus been deprived of the benefits which the now unused ganglions could have given him.

One of these ganglions was directly concerned with divine vision.

Through hypnotism we can, once again, rouse this ganglion. As a result we can see the facts of the future life which, at this stage, remain invisible to us.

Endowed with divine vision one can see one's future much in the same way as one sees movies in ones room.

Hypnotism has a proven capacity to rouse similarly many dormant ganglions and obtain greater capabilities. He can clearly see into the future. Thus he can rise higher and anticipate future threats.

IMPACT ON SPEECH

Through hypnotism we can very easily influence our voice. Often we come across such people as have rich personality and yet being stammerers they do not create any good and lasting impact on others. There is something incomplete in their personality.

Through hypnotism one can gain control over such deficiencies. While being put to hypnotic sleep the 'medium' could be suggested that his voice is quite sound, he can pronounce words accurately and whatever stammer he had in his voice is now gone and when he will wake up he will never stammer.

It is nothing but a mental effect. For when it goes into his inner mind that he cannot talk straight and properly, he develops a certain degree of diffidence which ultimately causes stammering. However, when the 'subject' is suggested during his hypnotic sleep that his voice does not have any stammering, his mental fear vanishes and once this fright is removed, his voice develops into an effective, impressive and straight instrument.

IMPACT ON PULSE RATE

Medical scientists have always held that a healthy human body has a stable pulse rate. If at all it registers a very low or very high rate, the individual falls sick.

Often the big spurt in the pulse rate is due to blood pressure. Similarly when one is furious or frightened the pulse rate registers a sharp decline. At times the pulse rate shoots up to a dangerous degree with the result that it proves fatal.

According to medical scientists there is no medicine which has a proven capacity to bring a measure of stability in the pulse rate. It is only by a steady application one can bring stability to the pulse rate.

However, hypnotism can bring pulse rate under effective control all at once. The 'medium' is put to hypnotic sleep and then he is suggested that whatever anger or panic he had in him is now gone. As a result he is much better than before.

Put to such experiments the human body goes through a series of awe-provoking changes and ultimately the pulse rate is brought under effective control.

If viewed from a different angle, one may see that the pulse rate is directly related to the breathing system. In such a situation if we control our breathing we can also control our pulse rate.

Under hypnotic influence the breathing remains under effective control. One also controls one's breathing, through *pranayams*, which is the base of hypnotism. An efficient hypnotist can never have an irregular pulse rate.

IMPROVEMENT IN HEARING

Hypnotism makes a powerful impact on one's hearing capacity. There are many including children who are hard of hearing. As a result they do not feel a completeness in their making.

Under hypnotic spell the ganglions and related senses which otherwise remain inactive get effectively activated. One develops the hearing defect because the ganglions remain inactive normally.

The ganglions and related senses can be strengthened through hypnotism. It, therefore, brings about a corresponding increase in one's hearing capacity.

I have myself conducted various experiments in this field. I got success in every attempt. I am, therefore, in a position to say that one's hearing capacity can be strengthened through hypnotism and thus the big defect in his personality can be removed.

ROLE IN STRENGTHENING OF VOLITION

Man is prone to thinking. Always he thinks including when he is asleep. When he is sleeping his inner mind remains very active. One can, thus, see desires and inclinations play a vital role in one's life.

Man feels happy when some of his desires get fulfilled. But when he finds some of his desires are not being fulfilled, he ponders over them and feels terribly aggrieved.

As we have already discussed earlier a strong personality exercises a good measure of restraint over his desires. He, in fact, dominates his desires. He fulfils his desires by conscious efforts and hard work.

The individual's success is commensurate with the degree of his will-power. It is likely to achieve glory if he has a strong will-power. It is due to will-power man is ever ready to suffer any personal pain. He climbs to the top of the Himalayas by virtue of will-power. He crosses the limitless ocean and the vast expanse of the Sahara desert all because of the will-power. It is a pointer to his strong will-power.

However, the individual who is weak-willed is not able to do anything in his life. He remains an ordinary man. At every stage he encounters defeat, humiliation and indifference.

A spurt in the will-power gets the individual a particular kind of power. It helps him advance in life. If he remains weak-willed, he will never experience the particular kind of energy. For this reason he does not develop any dynamism. He does not progress in his life.

Through hypnotism we can strengthen and develop our

will-power. As a result we shall have in us the special power developing, which is likely to take us to greater success and bigger advances.

ROLE IN THOUGHT CONCENTRATION

The mind is prone to wayward movements. It is only when we gain a measure of control over the mind that we can make the mind work for success.

In the *Ramayana* we have read that the grief-stricken Sita used to be completely engrossed in thoughts centring around Rama while she was in exile in the garden belonging to Ravana, her husband's adversary. She would not hear the footsteps of the persons coming close. Nor would she get disturbed by the din and noise around. The principal reason of this imperturbability was her engrossment in the sequence of her thoughts.

Normally we begin to go deep in thinking at a certain point of concentration. We achieve a lot when we succeed in reaching the depths.

WEIGHTLESSNESS

During hypnotic trance one does not feel the weight of any object. For the individual in that state remains in a special kind of frame. If you put upon the hypnotised body a heavy object— say of 40 kgs, he will not feel the weight of it.

Through the medium of hypnotism one can develop one's capacity to bear and carry such heavy objects which normally he cannot.

TASTELESSNESS

During hypnotic trance one cannot ascertain the taste of anything. For instance, you offer grapes to your 'subject' and suggest that he is eating pebbles. He will at once spit it out. He will really feel as though he has pebbles in his mouth.

Many persons have aversion for certain objects. After bringing them to hypnotic trance if you suggest that those objects are likeable and that he should eat them, he will start liking and eating them. The aversion will certainly go. Now he will start relishing those objects for which he had aversion.

KNOWLEDGE OF GESTATION

Indian *yogis* used to know all about gestation period by virtue of their extraordinary spiritual powers. Now it is no more a miraculous affair. For hypnotism invokes the past to the 'medium' and also full knowledge about his gestation. For after the fourth month of conception the foetus develops into a full-fledged embryo throbbing with inner life. As a result it records all incidents from the fourth month onwards to its birth time. These incidents concern its mother-her sorrows, worries, troubles get recorded in the life within the womb, whose inner mind begins to receive the total impact of all these incidents.

Through hypnotism one could, therefore, ascertain a certain knowledge about all the incidents which made impact on the life within the womb. We could also have a fair idea of the personality of the concerned individual.

SCHOOLING IN THE WOMB

In Hindu mythology we have read about Abhimanyu who in the womb had learnt from his father how to cut through the wheel-shaped battle-order. In the Mahabharata war when Arjuna was outside the battle arena the onus of breaking through the wheel-shaped battle-order devolved on Abhimanyu. He said he knew the art of breaking through this kind of battle-order, but he did not know the strategy of coming out of the battle-order. For he said he in his womb had learnt the art of breaking through this kind of battle-order and yet as his father was instructing his mother on the strategy of coming out of this battle order, she had fallen asleep. As a result Abhimanyu, too, fell asleep in the womb. So he could not learn the strategy of coming out of the battle-order.

The meaning is quite clear. Thoughts make their own impact on the life within the womb through its mother. And if one so chooses, one could instruct the foetus in the womb. During hypnotic sleep the external mind of the mother remains asleep. But her inner mind even in that state remains quite active and is in a position to receive all suggestions and influences.

Accordingly, if the mother during her hypnotic sleep is instructed in various aspects of knowledge, the foetus will accept this knowledge and remember it even after birth.

For instance, I made a couple go through an experiment. Both husband and wife were very pious, known for their high principles of conduct and adherence to the best customs. They sought to give birth to a child who would be as virtuous and ideal. When the wife conceived, they followed my suggestion and began to live at Hardwar on the banks of the river Ganga.

I had taught the husband the complexities of hypnotism. So every afternoon he would put his wife to hypnotic sleep and recite in sweet and sonorous accents extracts from the *Ramayana* and give her instructions in religion and scriptures. For five months he continued to practise like this. Every morning and evening they would go out to the river bank and converse mostly on religion.

A boy was born to them. The couple lived there for about five years. The boy was brought up in the highest religious traditions. He was kept away from the pollution of modern ways.

The boy was hardly five years old when he began to hold spiritual discourses like an erudite scholar. He knew many Sanskrit couplets and his oration was very impressive. Indeed it was a miracle that a tiny-tot hardly 5 years old should discuss recondite principles of religion with such authority. From long distances people flocked about to have a view of this prodigy. They were struck-dumb.

The couple is still alive. Of course their son too. It is unique that he should have such profound knowledge at his age.

It is true that the foetus in the womb participates in instructions. It remains stable for all time to come.

PRE-NATAL MEMORIES

Experts of hypnotism hold that they can know about one's previous life or lives through the medium of hypnotism. What was our life before the present life? What was our basic faith? To know answers to these questions is important, for the present life is not a separate entity. It is continuous with our previous life. The life we had and the activities in which we participated in the life or lives prior to the present life are bound to leave a massive impact on our present life. In case we want to know all about our present life we should know as much as possible of the previous life or lives.

According to Indian philosophy the present life is but a ring in a long chain. The previous life was also a ring and the life to come will also be a ring. All these rings make a long chain. Unless we know all about the chain, we cannot know the rings separately. It is, therefore, essential that we know all the rings—the previous and the following—through a sound knowledge of hypnotism.

In hypnotic trance the inner mind goes thought-free as also stoical. But the speed of the inner mind in this state is terrific indeed. If the inner mind is suggested in such a state, one can know all about the previous life. Similarly through hypnotism we can also know all about the life to follow—where we will be born and what we will be and all that.

Viewed objectively the science of hypnotism has reached a high stage of development in the modern age. It has proved its capacity to make the human life very comfortable and happy. Through the instrumentality of hypnotism we can concentrate our thought and reach greater heights. And through a proper cultivation of the will-power we can achieve a rare integrity.

Indeed all credit must go to the human life which can reach its goal within such a short time.

For the purpose of reaching its goal, it needs the co-operation of various forces. Hypnotism ranks very high in these life-giving forces. With the help of this science we can overcome our own deficiencies and create in our personality an extra-ordinary attraction for others. While we can influence others, we can reshape our own personality into a powerful instrument of good health as influential as impressive.

The need of the hour is that we make a systematic study of this science, and taking advantage of its special powers we reach the goal of integrity.

SPIRITUAL POWERS

Basically hypnotism is the science of the mind and the brain. It is the only science which ensures dissociation of thoughts from the mind and the brain. It is, again, this science that can invest integrity to our life, besides helping it to advance towards its chosen goal.

Hypnotism has been the oldest and the most significant science of India. It was the sages and seers of yore who gave us this remarkable science. Through the medium of this science they have attained such *siddhis*[1] as are truly incredible. They solved such complex and difficult problems as were beyond the power of the most competent.

When the mind has reached *turiyawastha*[2] the practitioner claims title to the *ashta-siddhis*[3] and he automatically prevails over the not-so-important meditations. In the ancient scriptures we have come across the instances of *yogis* who walk on the surging waves of the ocean, who could fly with the winds, and who could view things thousands of miles away. To us these achievements have come down as miracles. But for the Indian seers of yore these were accomplishments made possible as a result of their achieved capability to gain full control over the mind and bring about total dissociation of thoughts and mind and also acquire a certain competence to awaken the inner mind. It is by way of this rigorous restraint that they brought off such incredible accomplishments..

Faith has been the bed-rock of every meditation. One cannot hope to achieve anything without faith. Lord Krishna Himself said:

SHRADHADAN LABHATE GYANMAH. If you have faith you can certainly succeed in your life. It is only faith which gives rise to the need to forge bonds with others. Faith has never been skin-deep. It needs a specific temperament. We long to share a few moments of the other person, which, so to say, has been the genesis of faith.

A beautiful woman having had to live at a solitary place will not find herself secure. Even the presence of half-a-dozen men will not remove the substance of her deepening insecurity. She would, however, feel totally secure in the company of her

---

1. *Siddhis:* Attainment of divine grace and spiritual salvation.
2. *Turiyawastha*: Explained elsewhere.
3. *Ashta-Siddhis:* There are in all eight *siddhis*.

husband. The basic reason is that she has implicit faith in her husband. She does not have the same faith in others regardless of their protestations.

A similar faith operates between the teacher and the disciple. If the disciple does not have any faith for his teacher, he will not have the basic ingredient to learn anything from him. Endowed with this ingredient he can hope to learn everything from his teacher.

A teacher has about twenty disciples. It is only a few of them who achieve everything within the prescribed time. Their success is always attributed to their ingrained faith in their teacher. No faith, no knowledge.

As we have discussed earlier, the thoughts which keep on coming up in our mind necessarily make an impact on the person sitting opposite. It is not, in any case, a one-way traffic. We, too, come under the impact of the thoughts surging in the mind of the person opposite. So the process evidently is reciprocal. For instance, if we are sceptical of the teacher's learning and we continue to question his competence, our unspoken doubts will elicit in the teacher a similar reaction, with the result that he will lose all interest in imparting knowledge on the scale he had wanted to do.

Assailed by unfaith and disbelief we find it impossible to concentrate all our attention on the *mantra*. When the *mantra* is not spared our exclusive concentration, we will not achieve what we wanted from this meditation.

Earlier, we have emphasised that a stoical mind *viz.* a mind having witnessed its total dissociation with thoughts and ideas has always been taken as the ultimate achievement of the human life. This kind of mind has always been necessary for the accomplishment of any meditation whatsoever. Without such dissociation the mind is normally reduced to a crowded place and the life to its very ordinary and mundane level. Dissociation is the first condition if we want to develop our inherent capacity to bring off the *mantra* alive.

It is, again through this process that one reaches closer to the Almighty. For you have only one predominant concentration, which proves fully effective. You must however, take note of the fact that insolence and arrogance have always been our adversaries. In fact, egotism has always been subversive. It has always weakened our concentration. On the other hand, your meditation should be an exercise in humility. Knowledge must not lead to power. You must always show an awareness of the fact that such knowledge has been the forte of many predecessors and you are an heir to their acquisition, which yet remains unsurpassed. This kind of generalisation must remain the only accomplishment of your life.

Arrogance and pride make a man restless. It destroys one's makeup for contentment.

In the following pages I should like to discuss a few distinguished *siddhis* which are based on hypnotism. One who attains a proven proficiency in hypnotism can also attain these *siddhis*.

It is not at' all necessary that one must succeed in the very initial attempt. Failure must not put you off. You have to reflect calmly and coolly where you have some wrong and what have been the reasons of your failure.

So many times we do not succeed even after repeated attempts. The basic reason is the instability in the mind. For all success and all failure entirely depend on one's quality of mind. You must, therefore, forge ahead to gain a better control over your mind.

We are also social beings. We cannot escape our social responsibilities and obligations. As a result we are always beset with various kinds of concerns. In a state of mind like this, it is not always possible to concentrate all our attention at one single point. The day we are really involved in all kinds of concerns, it is better we give up the practice of meditation on that day. For as experience shows the mind has to struggle a lot to dissociate itself from concerns. It will involve a continuous struggle, which, in any case, is not congenial to the mind.

1. VICHAR SANKRAMAN SIDDHI[1]

By this *siddhi* we mean a capacity to transmit our thoughts into others. In other words, the other person should do what we want him to do, although we would not say it.

The mind is never vacuous. Every moment a multitude of thoughts keep crowding about in the mind. As a result the thought on which we want to lay emphasis does not get emphasised and accordingly it does not create the requisite impact on others.

We have already told you about the two minds. In the conscious state the outer mind remains active. The inner mind being always alert and awake receives all ideas and images at all times.

Certain thoughts arise in our mind. Suppose they concern the man sitting opposite. In that case the pressure it generates must make an impact on his inner mind. So much so that he feels compelled to follow our unspoken thoughts. But the postulate for this sort of transmission requires us to have only stable and mature thoughts. It needs clear and workable ideas too. It is only then they will make a powerful impact on the inner mind of the person sitting opposite. He will accordingly begin to act up to our unspoken behest.

The thoughts you want to transmit must remain very firm and stable. It is possible only when we have in our mind only one preponderating thought. In that case we shall be able to transmit such a thought with full force and with full energy.

On the contrary, if you have your mind cluttered up with a crowd of all kinds of thoughts including the one you want to transmit to a certain person, it is very often seen that all thoughts are reduced to a common level including the one you wanted to transmit to a certain person seated opposite. Suppose you want to back up the one thought you seek to transmit with all force and energy. In that case your force and energy will get dissipated among the host of thoughts crowding about in your mind. The casualty is the thought you wanted to transmit. It does not get the force and energy which it needed.

It is, therefore, essential that you practise the technique of dissociating your mind from thoughts and ideas.

---

1. The literal meaning: The *siddhi* which ensures transmission of thoughts or ideas.

In the preceding pages we have discussed this technique in some detail.

It, however, needs a regular practice. Mornings and evenings are the best time for this practice.

Practising transmission of thoughts one should advance one's practice gradually and steadily. It is no use why you should feel disappointed and put off if you are not successful in your initial attempts. You are certain to be crowned with success if you continue to practise for some time.

I give you an example. Suppose you receive a guest at your home. I suggest you start your practice right from this point. In any case make sure that not a word and not a sound escapes your tongue.

In a few moments the guest desires to have some hot drinks. He is actually getting slightly fidgety for some drink. If he does so, it should be taken as a pointer to the right transmission of your thoughts.

Say, you are in your office. Now you work up a suggestion that your officer comes to your cabin with a certain file and he asks you to attend to the file. The officer is sitting in the cabin next to yours. You do not see him, for he is not seated opposite. Nevertheless you try to plant on his mind the idea which arose in your mind. Repeat it 5 to 7 times.

Take note of the fact that the speed of the transmitted thought depends entirely on your will-power. If you have a strong will-power, the thought gains in velocity. Also, there must be full concentration on the thought. A crowd of thoughts will dissipate your energy and take away your capacity to concentrate on the single thought. It simply does not get itself projected with any speed.

If you repeat the transmission of the thought for 10 to 15 times, you will see your officer himself will arrive in your cabin armed with the particular file. While handing over the file he would request you to attend to the file as a priority item. He was going out and so he thought he should assign you this work. If you achieve this you could take it as a pointer to your success in transmission of thoughts.

At the same time make sure that you should not entertain in your mind mutually contradictory thoughts at a certain given time. For instance, you are seeking to transmit the idea that the officer will come to your cabin with the file. At the same time if you start entertaining the idea that the officer being a higher person will in no case come to your table, this negative stance too will make its own impact on the said officer. The negative stance will certainly weaken your earlier positive stance. As a result there will be no effective force in the transmission of the thought.

It is, therefore, highly essential that you concentrate on a single thought and in no case entertain mutually contradictory thoughts.

In the preceding pages I have discussed the technique of *picture tratak* and *idol tratak*. If you want to succeed in this kind of concentration you should take resort to this kind of *tratak*. For when we practise *idol tratak* we invoke in front of us the idol which comes off alive. It is another thing that we have closed our eyes at that time.

Similarly when we seek to transmit our thoughts to a certain person, we should have his image alive in our view. Make sure that we also develop so much, of strength that no other image emerges before us to distract our attention from this image.

When the image or picture is invoked and it comes before your eyes, suggest or transmit the thought into the image. You will find that you have succeeded. In the example given earlier, the image of the officer must have come off alive in your eyes. It is only then transmission of thoughts is found to be feasible.

Suppose you have never seen the person to whom you are to transmit your thoughts. In this case, obtain his photograph or picture. If it is not available, try to construct a semblance of the person from whatever you have been told about him. Give it a concrete form and then try to transmit your thoughts to the form or picture as the case may be. You will succeed in this experiment.

Once a certain gentleman came to me whose son was absconding. He belonged to a village. So he did not have any photograph of his son. He urged me to devise a way so that the boy developed a sound conduct and he came back home at the earliest. The boy had developed a sort of aversion for his home.

Facing a situation like this I had no other way than to collect details about the appearance of the boy. The gentleman told me all about his son's colour, height, face structure and dress. I constructed an image which came to resemble his son.

Now I stabilised the image in my mind. With all force at my command I suggested to him that he must come back home at the earliest. He returned home without any delay. The aversion that he had developed for the other members of his family was due to unfounded doubts in him. The doubts had no basis whatsoever. He must, therefore, come back.

For over 15 minutes I kept on transmitting the thought. Later I saw his father off. No wonder that the boy went back home on the third day. Reaching home he told his parents that he felt as though somebody exactly three days ago was calling him to go back home. And he called repeatedly. The voice rang in his ears continuously. It kept ringing in his ears whether he was awake or asleep. As a result, he had to come back.

What I mean to say is: If you have a very strong will-power and a developed capacity to transmit your thoughts, it is certain that the thrust of the thoughts will be felt by the picture whether the person is sitting before you or he is some thousands of miles away.

Initially you could take to certain practices to ascertain whether you are treading on the right path.

1. Experiment it on a member of your family. Ask him to get you a tumbler of water at once. To work on this experiment you should be seated in a quiet room, close your eyes and invoke the image of that person in front of your eyes.

   Now transmit the thought that he gets you water at once.

   After some time you will see that the person is standing before you with a tumbler of water. The fact is that you had not asked him to do the errand. When you tell him that you had never asked him to do this errand, he will feel really surprised. He would say he thought I was asking for water.

Any success in an experiment like this will be deemed to be a big step forward.

2. Now you widen your area of operation. Invoke the image of somebody who lives in the same town. Transmit the thought that he should phone you at this moment.

You keep on transmitting this thought for 10 to 15 minutes. You will find the telephone calls exactly at the same time. At the other end is the same person whose image you had invoked in front of your eyes.

Initially you will take 10 to 15 minutes to transmit a certain thought. Gradually you will develop the capacity to accomplish the same thing taking not more than a minute. You will be able to transmit the entire thrust and make him do whenever you might want.

3. Now widen your area of operation still more. Choose somebody whether a friend of your own son or wife living in some other town. Transmit the idea that he should write to you immediately. Suggest to him to write on a certain particular matter of your interest. It is again you who have to tell him what matter he will choose to write on. For instance, you transmit the thought that he should write how he has been longing to see you. He will ask you to visit his place at once.

When you have transmitted the thought, do not forget to take down the day and the date of its despatch. Now you wait for the letter. You will see from the date of the letter that it was written on the same date when you transmitted your thought.

Similarly you can transmit your thought to friends and relatives living abroad and make them do anything you might desire.

4. When you have gone through a certain course of practice you get hold of the photograph or picture of an unknown person. Transmit your thoughts to the person and make the photograph or picture of the 'medium' for this purpose.

Ask him to do a set of jobs.

When he has done the jobs as you suggested, it should be taken as a pointer to your further advance in the field.

5. Now you try to transmit thoughts to an unknown person whom you have never seen and whose photograph or picture you do not have. You have only been told of a broad profile of that person. Construct his image and transmit thoughts to the unknown person through the image.

Success in this experiment will establish you as an outstanding hypnotist.

We would like to offer you a few words of caution. It is necessary that you follow the full import of the caution.

1. At the initial stage you take to practice at 10 or 11 at night. For at this time the outer mind of the target person remains asleep and the inner mind goes active to the maximum. As a result whatever thoughts you would like to transmit will make a swift and powerful impact on his mind. You will have a quicker success.

2. At this time you, too, feel very peaceful. You find peace all around. There is no din and bustle around. The atmosphere is highly amenable. So all practitioners will find this time very suitable.

3. Do not indulge in anti-social and unethical activities through this medium. If you want to lead astray a woman of sterling character through this medium, the act will be taken as positively anti-social. You will not get any success. For the mind of such a woman is strong enough. Your thoughts will collide against her mind.

4. You must put this accomplishment only to noble ends. For instance, your friend's son is not inclined to study. He has shunned all reading and writing. You could take him back to studies. Through transmission of thoughts you could make him concentrate his attention on studies.

5. We have already said that one could succeed in this technique only when one feels blissfully peaceful. No other thoughts must cross your mind. Your mind will entertain

only one thought. There will be no mutually contrary thoughts. Your will-power will remain very strong. It needs a tremendous concentration. It is only then you may succeed.

6. Faith is basic to all such activities. If you do not have any faith in this meditation or if you do not have any confidence in this activity you will not have any success, howsoever you may try. For the contrary thoughts have already taken hold of your mind. The thought was that all this is futile and it is not simply possible to achieve what is being suggested.

Once Jesus Christ told his disciples that the hill opposite might find itself uprooted and get submerged in the ocean beyond, should they wish it so with a certain measure of devotion. But one can accomplish it only when one has undivided faith. In this symbolic one sentence Jesus Christ has said everything about faith. He has further said that one can accomplish impossible things if one has full and unshakable faith. Your mind feels inclined to address itself to the task with full speed and total absorption. So faith is basic to any success in meditation.

The *siddhi* ensuring transmission of thoughts has been found to be unique. We can be masters of the universe. We can make any person amenable. We can thus make others feel happier and more prosperous.

2. SANKALPA SADHANA[1]

The practice of taking a solemn vow has been of greatest significance in our life. In the Indian *yogic* philosophy both cultivation of will-power and meditation seeking to reiterate the vow have taken a very prominent place. For it is widely accepted that nobody can progress without developing these crucial faculties.

Everybody nurses deep within himself an ambition. Somebody wants to be a millionaire. There is another who wants to get rid of the chronic disease he is suffering from. He wants his physique to emerge extraordinarily beautiful. There are others who want to achieve godhood.

However it is only the fortunate few who realise their ambition in their life. Others remain content with the retrace it involves. Most people make do with the ambitions remaining beyond their reach.

The principal reason of non-fulfilment of ambitions is the big deficiency in one's volition. The weaker you are in volition, the farther you are from your target.

Almost daily we hit upon brand new plans and ideas. We remain engrossed in the latest plans and ideas, for we want to achieve something in our life. Our plans and ideas end up in castles which we seek to build in the air. They end up like this because they are not backed up with a necessary measure of will-power and volition. We must have a sense of determination. We must resolve that whatever we decide, we stick to it and we will achieve it come what may. If with this determination we go ahead we will certainly succeed.

I would like to emphasise that we should have realistic plans in our life. Besides, the plans must be relative. Its determinants should be time, age and agency. Suppose we resolve that we shall bring New York to the neighbourhood of New Delhi. A plan like this is bound to end up as an exercise in futility. For it violates the determinants of time and space. Suppose somebody plans to confront a modern war with the help of swords. It will not work in this age of science. It will remain a historical anachronism. Surely we cannot hope to relapse into primitive times.

It is, therefore, essential that we should plan after careful thinking. If a poor person aspires to be a millionaire within three months, he will certainly come to grief. One can always have a determination to earn more within a certain framework. There is nothing wrong to have a determination like this.

Planning must precede determination. We should, however, plan in a practical way. So when you have evolved a realistic plan, you better take it down on a piece of paper. You should take a

---

1. *Sankalpa* means resolve or determination. The Hindus take a solemn vow at the start of a religious ceremony reiterating the purpose for which it is intended.

vow that you will achieve this plan and that you will devote all your efforts and time to this end.

You must now train your sights on achieving this target. No doubt you will come across all kinds of hurdles at every step. At times, poised against adversary condition your determination will slacken. But there is nothing to feel defeated. You should dedicate yourself with a redoubled vigour. Your determination must remain as grim as it was initially. You will achieve your target within the scheduled time.

Once I wanted to perform meditation. For this purpose I needed an *asana*[1] made of the skin of a black deer. It was not available in my town.

In the evening I resolved to have this meditation from the next afternoon. Although I did not have the *asana* I was positive I would have the meditation at the appointed time.

The next morning I saw, to my great surprise, a disciple of mine bringing from Varanasi the *asana* I needed. He said he had longed to present me an *asana* like this for a long time. Now that he suddenly got it, he thought he should present it to me.

I could have my meditation at the appointed hour. It reinforced my feeling that one can have anything done if one's determination remains firm.

Once I was sitting in the *asrama*[1] of a fellow disciple. It was located in a forest, within a kilometre from the town. He ran short of *dhoop*[2], an ingredient of worship. He wanted me to fetch it from the town. It was chilly winter and so I was extremely reluctant to go out. He understood my feelings. He assured me that I need not go out. He was quite confident that it would be made available by some disciple before long.

It was really amazing that soon a devotee came to the *asrama* with a packet of incense.

It should suffice to offer the instance of St. Philmore, a famous American saint. Once he ran out of food stock. He had in his *asrama* over 50 children, mostly orphans. The children were between 5 and 15 years old.

---

1. *Asana:* A seat for meditation made of skin, wool, cotton or grass.

As a rule the children ate their lunch at 11 a.m. That day it was already half past ten. The manager asked the saint what was to be done to face the situation. Meanwhile no food stock was procured. Neither was any other arrangement made.

Almost imperturbably the saint said in reply: Serve them lunch at 11 a.m.

He said to the manager that he need not to worry. The children would get their lunch at the appointed hour. They must eat their lunch.

The manager went back. Now it was five minutes to eleven. He came to the saint again. He said: Shall I ring the lunch bell? Shall I place before the children empty plates?

The saint said: Do ring the bell at the appointed hour. Let all children come to the dining hall.

Indeed the manager was greatly puzzled. He was quite worked up. Exactly at 11 he rang the lunch bell.

The children ran out from their rooms and converged in the dining hall.

Exactly at this time a van fully stocked with food supplies arrived at the *asrama*. A certain gentleman brought it to the *asrama*.

He said: I had ordered lunch for a hundred persons. They cooked it for two hundred persons. So I thought that I should feed the children.

The saint let him feed the children.

At 1 p.m. the saint sent for the manager. He asked him whether all children had had their lunch. The manager said that not only the children, but the entire staff had taken their lunch.

The saint said: Okay. I am releasing you from service from today. For you do not seem to have any faith in God. Nor do you have any firm resolve. You seemed to have faltered today. When the children always got their lunch at 11 a.m., what was the special worry today?

---

1. *Asrama:* Hermitage.
2. *Dhoop:* Incense. When the Hindus worship, they perfume the place with incense.

This incident, I should like to emphasise, exemplifies the importance of determination. Nothing could deter us if we are determined. The resolve must remain unshaken.

In the West they undertook much research in volition. They followed another technique. For instance, they write their wish on a piece of paper. They place it on their table. Everyday they concentrate their attention on this note for five minutes. Thus they focus their attention on the sentence written on the piece of paper. They continue to do like this for a month. Then they tear the paper into pieces and throw them away.

They believe they get things done in this manner. For it is true the full force of the mind projects itself on the paper for one full month. It enriches volition and enables it to reach the target.

Although one derives success from this technique, I would not think that it is a perfect technique. The techniques which I discussed in the preceding lines are more authentic and more appropriate. They are better equipped to reach us to our destination.

Volition has been central to our life and to our success in life. The more we succeed in cultivating this faculty the closer we reach the destination.

It is through the practice of *sankalpa* that we can attain completeness in life.

3. DOORDARSHANA[1] SIDDHI

Doordarshana gives us the *siddhi* or accomplishment to see things beyond time and space and put it down as it is.

As I have already explained earlier, God has endowed man with remarkable power and limitless potential. What is more, man has within him an inner mind which is not determined by any constraints whatsoever. The inner mind is transcendental. Besides seeing the present it can peep into past and see clearly all past incidents said to have taken place more than a thousand years ago. Similarly he can see into future and establish live relations with the milestone of the future.

Being in no way controlled by the usual determinants of time and space the inner mind is a separate sovereign entity. It has a tremendous velocity. It travels more than a thousand miles per second. It travels into the past as well as into the future with equal facility.

No doubt the modern science has acknowledged the existence of the inner mind and also that it is unique by itself. At the same time one wonders whether science has been able to explore its remarkable potential. It may take yet thousands of years to do so.

The outer mind is conditioned by contemporary incidents. The inner mind, however, is not at all conditioned by anything. It remains immune to contemporary developments. It has, therefore, a greater measure of freedom and quietude. It is only through an appropriate cultivation of the inner mind that we can attain *doordarshana siddhi.*

This kind of clairvoyance is also possible through *Karma Pishachini Siddhi*[1]. It, however, enables one to see only the past, and not the future.

In any case we are discussing here only hypnotism. It is through this medium that one can rouse the inner mind and see both past and future in a satisfactory way. It involves an active meditation and total and undivided concentration.

To practise *doordarshana sadhana* take a piece of glass 8" by 8". Use the soot of camphor to blacken its one side. Make sure that the glass on one side only is made black. Now place it on a table against the wall so that the black side faces you. Keep it at your eye-level atleast two feet away from where you are sitting. Spread out your *asana* and be seated in the best possible spirits.

Place a lamp[2] before the glass and light it. Close all doors and windows of the room. Now cool and collected, you fix your eye on the reflected flame in the glass. Make sure that you do not see anything other than the flame.

You breathe very slowly. If you breathe hard it may disturb the flame. You must have full control over your breathing.

Practise like this for some time or, if necessary, for a few days. You will gradually see that the black side is getting lighted.

---

1. *Doordarshana:* Clairvoyance.

If you can really see it lighted, you could take it as a positive sign of your success. The light on the black side of the glass is actually the light of your own inner mind which gets reflected on the glass.

Similarly you make this practice regular. After some time you will begin to see many sights in that portion of the glass. Now you must be more careful, for it indicates that the outer mind and the inner mind are getting in touch with each other, and that whatever the outer mind is experiencing, it is transmitting the felt experiences to the inner mind.

Now try to see in it the sights or places which you have seen before. For instance, try for a moment to think what is taking place outside the main door of the Taj Mahal.

When you think so the outer mind will immediately transmit this message to the inner mind. As a result the inner mind will try to see for a moment what all is taking place at the main door of the Taj Mahal. You will feel totally surprised to clearly see the Taj Mahal, the main door of this monument and also the crowd moving about.

You had better keep to this practice regularly and try to see sights and places situated far away.

Your eyes will not help in this field. When you close your eyes, the minds eye or the inner eye opens up. It is this eye which seeks to see all such sights.

The glass piece which you used was only for initial practice. After you achieve success it will serve no use. For the inner mind wakes up the moment you close your eyes and be seated in all tranquillity. It will begin to see objects and incidents far away.

This practice looks easy apparently. It is not, however, that easy. It needs a lot of efforts, much hard work and total meditation.

---

1. *Karma Pishachini Siddhi:* It is an *aghor* practice. Protagonists of the *aghor* path claim allegiance to Lord Siva. Their main job is to charm the soul of the dead person. Literally the word *aghor* means not terrible. But the rites which they follow are dreadful, perhaps abominable also to an extent. It cannot, therefore, be recommended for universal practice.

2. The Indian practice is to use *ghee*—clarified butter preferably of cow's milk)—for oil in the lamp for such religious purposes.

But there cannot be any two opinions that the practitioner will eventually succeed, should he keep to a persistent practice of this exercise.

We can also see the past of the person sitting opposite. We can see what all transpired in his past, and what actually took place on a certain date. We can also see what is in store for him in the future.

Suppose the person is not present around. We can obtain his photograph and see his past and future.

In this meditation distance does not count. In a moment we can see what is happening beyond hundreds of thousands of miles. Similarly we can flit into the past as well as the future.

The initial stage needs a long, protracted practice. After he had gone through a successful practice the practitioner begins to see all such sights and locations as he might want to see, the moment he sits on his *asana* with a calm and tranquil mind.

4. BHAVISHYA KAL SIDDHI[1]

You could call this *siddhi* as future time meditation. It is akin to the clairvoyance method we have discussed in the preceding paragraph. As with the earlier technique one could, following this technique, see as well into one's past as well as future. In one important aspect it is, however, quite distinct from any of the techniques described elsewhere. Following this technique the predictions one makes are generally found to be more authentic and correct.

Astrology for what we know is given to making predictions. It has its own limitations, for it ensures the services of only the outer mind. And by now we have known pretty well that the outer mind being involved in the pressures being built by external contemporary happenings is not totally free. A mind vitiated by such pressures cannot be fully relied upon for making correct and objective predictions.

There is another limitation to the science of astrology. Astrology like any other science is not complete in itself. Besides, the canvas of astrology is limitless. It is, therefore, prone to commit mistakes. Suppose as many as ten astrologers study a particular horoscope. Obviously they will make ten sets of predictions.

Possibly one or two might feel vindicated while the rest might go wrong.

Until you involve the active co-operation of the inner mind in making predictions, the job of making predictions will remain incomplete and inaccurate. In the example referred to in the foregoing paragraph we have referred to the correct predictions of one or two astrologers. Their predictions proved to be correct because both the outer and the inner minds chanced to co-operate in this job.

If at all we succeed in involving in astrological calculations the active co-operation of the inner mind, the predictions such as we make might prove to be more accurate and authentic.

Once I was studying the horoscope of a very poor man. 1 felt from the reading that the person must be very ordinary, for there were no special planetary movements in his horoscope.

Later when I closed my eyes and concentrated upon my outer and inner minds I discovered that the person was not at all that ordinary. Indeed he appeared to be dressed in a very common apparel. But he was very opulent and he represented a high social class.

I opened my eyes and told the person that he looked a very ordinary person as per his horoscope. I also told him that when I studied deeper I found that he was indeed a very opulent person and that he must be having millions.

For a minute or two the person kept looking at me. Then he conceded that I was correct. He owned a well-established cotton mill. He changed over into ordinary dress only to test me, he said.

We often find perhaps our own eyes can at times cheat us. For the obvious limitations of astrology, the predictions it makes can go wrong and often incomplete. But in no case does the inner mind commit any wrong. Whatever it sees and whatever it experiences is all complete in itself leaving no scope for any error or mistake.

It is, therefore, appropriate that the persons who want to be experts to making predictions should turn their attention to

---

1. *Bhavishya Kal Siddhi*: It is chiefly the technique to predict the future of a certain person.

the inner mind and develop it as much as possible and study predictions with the insights placed at our disposal by the inner mind. Perhaps only then can our predictions prove to be accurate.

5. KRITYA[1] SIDDHI

In Hindu mythology and scriptures we have often come across references to the fact that poised against danger the gods or the demons by virtue of their own *yogic* force used to create an extraordinarily endowed male or female and have it subserve their jobs. Lord Siva was unable to destroy the *Daksha Yajna*[1] To meet this situation he created an earthly being—*Kritya* and destroyed the *yajna* and killed *Daksha*[2].

We come across many more similar references in *Devi Bhagwat*[3].

When all gods felt totally exasperated by the oppression let loose by *Bhasmasur*, Lord Vishnu created an enchanting woman—*Kritya* who wrought enchantment on *Bhasmasur* and finished him off.

Kritya, to put it short, is such an extraordinarily endowed woman who gets done even impossible things. She is unique in the sense she defies classification. She does not belong to the order of gods nor to the underworld of demons nor to any other known category. Strictly speaking she is created by force of one's own mental strength and determination. She is our mental creation—a child of our inner mental integrity.

The meditation which gets us this power is unique by all standards. It is kept by and large undisclosed. And yet we would like to divulge it for the knowledge of our readers.

The practitioners should do well to remember that they should regularly take their seat at one appointed place. All doors and windows of the room should remain closed. Care should be taken to ensure perfect peace in the room.

Early in the morning the practitioner should take to this exercise. The most propitious time for this practice is just one hour before

---

1. *Kritya:* In India's heritage *Kritya* is said to be an extraordinarily endowed entity assuming the form of either woman or man created not biologically but by the force generated by *yoga*. It could be made to do impossible feats involving deeds of great bravery or seductive jobs of enchantment only for the mere impersonal ends.

the sunrise and one hour after the sunset.

With perfect tranquillity the practitioner must take his *asana* and imagine that a brilliant light is emanating from all parts of his body, contributing to the formation of the head of the mental girl. Similarly he will see that her hands, feet and other limbs are gradually assuming form and shape.

When he keeps his eyes closed for some more time the practitioner will clearly see the girl of his mental creation emerging from his own body. The practitioner must always remember that he keeps his concentration on the girl either by way of fixing his eye on her or by deeply thinking only of her. For not a single moment shall he deflect his attention from the creation emerging from his own body.

The practitioner may devote 4 to 6 months in this practice. If he sticks to this practice regularly he will find the mental girl always hovering about in his view. After some practice whether he is sleeping or travelling or meditating he will continue to see her in front of him. This mental child is none else than *Kritya*, who is endowed with greatest strength and valour. She is a power which knows no limits. She can accomplish impossible deeds. There is much difference between the human capacity and the capacity of *Kritya*. The human being was created out of five elements, while *Kritya* is created out of three elements. For this reason she has an extraordinary force and speed. Even the inner mind does not travel with that velocity.

When the image of *Kritya* remains settled down in front of you for all 24 hours, you could presume to have actually created *Kritya*.

Ask her to do anything. Ask her to fetch you something from Delhi this minute. She will get you the thing that minute. For instance, you have gone to a place 50 miles away from your

---

1. *Daksha Yajna:* Mythologically a religious feast held by *Daksha* in which Siva was not invited and was publicly abused, and Sati, the wife of Siva, could not stand this and died of grief when Siva came with his followers to the feast and spoiled it.

2. *Daksha: Daksha* is the father of Sati, Siva's wife.

3. *Devi Bhagwat: Bhagwat* is one of the *puranas* (Hindu mythology), an ancient holy book narrating the glory of Goddess Chandi, referred to as Devi.

house. Ask *Kritya* to fetch your diary which you had left behind at home. She gets you your diary in a moment. Not only these simple errands, you can also know the past as well as the future through the instrumentality of *Kritya*. For instance, you ask her to recount the past of somebody. She will narrate the whole thing in vivid details.

A remarkable point about *Kritya* is that you alone can hear her. You may be having a company of a dozen persons. Right in front of your company she will recount what she has been asked to find out. And yet you alone will hear her, and nobody else.

You can entrust her to do any command. Whether it is destruction of your enemy or something of personal benefit, she will get it done in a moment. But you will never allow her to stray away from your eye even for a moment. Make sure that you do not press her into service for ordinary and irrelevant errands. It is only when you are in a tight corner that you could make use of her services. The tasks which generally look humanly impossible should be assigned to her.

Indeed this *sadhana* is universally acknowledged as not only supreme but also unique by any standards.

∞

16. CONCLUSION

Hypnotism in itself is a complete and influential science. It has assumed a tremendous significance in the modern times. All other sciences are oriented towards materialism, while hypnotism alone is attuned to the mind. The principal object of this science is to heighten human consciousness so that the mind remains under effective control and proves its social orientation.

In human life the mind occupies a central position. For one may think of accomplishing any feat. What is essential is that the mind must offer its full co-operation to accomplish all kinds of feats. Today we see many happenings taking place all over the world. The mind has been central to all human initiatives. It is the mind which is chiefly instrumental in fomenting enmity and anger. Should the mind be put to a constructive use, we could have love, kindness, pity and piety prevailing all over, and so we could achieve world fraternity.

Indeed it is quite explicit that we could lessen and eliminate all kinds of socially subversive activities if we bring our mind under effective control. We could rather give encouragement to the socially useful activities.

In foreign countries this science has been accorded a very high place. They have begun to realise that this science has been basic to all human urges and initiatives. And in modern times, this science alone can make human life truthful, happy and glorious. In all other sciences we encounter contradictions. In hypnotism we do not see the spectre of contradictions arising. So they have started enlisting the co-operation of this science in every walk of life.

Hypnotism has brought about miracles in the world of medical treatment. Hypnotism has cured such diseases which people had given up as incurable. As far as psychic maladies are concerned, hypnotism has proved to be most effective. Hypnotism, as we already know, does not prescribe any medicines. It rather implants in the inner mind certain suggestions and cures all these complex and stubborn diseases by this method. We do not have any adverse reaction or side effects.

In human relations too, this science is being increasingly used. In the emerging new generation one notices an incomprehensible tendency of remaining dogmatic. One has treated several cases of such doggedness with the help of hypnotism. Drug-addicts have been liberated from their addiction. Even in common-place situation this science has proved to be very effective.

In India we have so far found little or no evidence of any extensive use of this science. Nor do we find any mass awakening getting organised through the instrumentality of this science. True we are occasionally using hypnotism is medical field, thanks to the Western impact. In any case we are not making use of this science in other fields in the way it should be done.

The Centre for the Study and Research in Indian Astrological Sciences, Jodhpur, has made a close appraisal of this situation in India and abroad. The Centre has found that shortly we shall lag behind all others if nothing is done to improve the present situation. By and large people in the West acknowledge the seminal job done by the Indians in this field. They accept that this science originated in India and if at all it has any potential to grow it is only India which can make it possible.

However, when we cast our eye on all sides we do not find the outlook promising. Many explorers from the West visit India to acquire some new knowledge in this field. They go back pretty dejected when they find nothing new and worthwhile in this field in this country.

If the deadlock remains as it is for some more time, perhaps we will feel compelled to go abroad to acquire even an elementary knowledge of this science.

A situation like this will surely be highly embarrassing for us, the Indians. This science is rooted in our soil and in our heritage. Despite this if we have no other way than to go abroad to learn this science, we will be faced with a shocking experience.

The Centre has gone into all these prospects in some depth. There should be a breakthrough, felt the Centre. We should initiate in our people a sense of confidence about this science and we should create a wide interest all over the country. It is only then they will be able to grasp the significance of this science, which in that case will begin to play a more effective and socially-oriented role.

As a sequel to our appraisal, the Centre has established an Academy of Hypnotism which works through the following major departments:

1. DEPARTMENT OF RESEARCH

The major thrust of a research in this department is to explore how best to use hypnotism more extensively and how effectively to realise all potential inherent in this science.

A relentless evaluation is also being undertaken. Many direct and oblique experiments are being conducted through the medium of this science so that the research findings are put to a severe verification continuously.

The department has come out with many remarkable findings in the field of study of the mind. The findings have been acknowledged all over the world.

2. DEPARTMENT OF PUBLICATIONS

After a close evaluation and objective verification of the research, the findings are published in journals so that ethers may derive profile from this latest knowledge.

The department publishes bulletins and journals. At the same time several rare ancient works have been recovered and published. Research findings are also published in separate volumes.

3. DEPARTMENT OF HEALING

This department is largely put to use for the purpose of treatment and healing. It is being increasingly used for treating psychic disorders. The results achieved in the department have been very outstanding.

The department organises evaluation, verification and codification of the insights gained in this field. The findings are published in volumes.

The department continues to receive several patients suffering from apparently incurable diseases. The department organises treatment of such patients.

The results have been very outstanding.

4. DEPARTMENT OF TEACHING

The department has organised teaching of this science. Anybody whether Indian or foreigner can join the courses. The department has taken up short-term courses and the learner can offer any of these courses and be admitted to the department.

There are no formal qualifications for admission to these courses. The department, however, seeks to ascertain whether the candidate has the basic capability and right interest in this field. The alumni who have successfully gone through these courses have earned reputation all over the country.

5. DEPARTMENT OF EXTRA-MURAL SERVICES

The department organises outside its campus seminars and symposia. Several times it organised a few seminars abroad too.

The department seeks to take up all such jobs concerning hypnotism which do not lend themselves for abroad classification under the major departments.

Although it has yet to vindicate itself with more work, the academy has already come in for a good measure by praise and commendation all over the world. Needless to say the Academy is the only institution of its kind. It has already brought out the only authentic and authoritative texts and research reports which have already engaged the scholarly attention of hypnotists all over the world.

OTHER IMPORTANT ACTIVITIES

The Academy has organised many other important activities, besides study and research of hypnotism. The activities have already earned the Academy scholarly attention all over the world. In several allied fields it has already earned high commendation of renowned scholars. We give below a mere introduction of the several activities the Academy has organised.

DEPARTMENT OF ASTROLOGY

The department undertakes to work out all kinds of astrological predictions. The work begins after obtaining the individual's date of birth, time of birth and place of birth. Those who have had their horoscopes duly drawn can send their horoscopes for astrological predictions. In case they do not have their horoscopes, they may send the prints of their both palms. They are advised to spread black ink on their palms and take impression on a white paper and send it up to the Academy.

The Department works out the facts and predictions of the entire life. It focuses its attention particularly on longevity, prospects in business, choice of trade, health, family, conjugal life, children, parents, friends and adversaries, job prospects, financial prospects and imminent obstacles in life. It also suggests ways and means to overcome the obstacle. Prospects of owning vehicle and house and going abroad are also studied.

The following jobs are also undertaken:

1. DETAILED REPLY TO ONE QUESTION

Any correspondent may ask one question for detailed answer. More than one question may also be asked. It is, however, essential that the correspondent sends in his horoscope or palmprints or photograph.

2. YEARLY PREDICTIONS

The Academy works out predictions for the whole year—what would be the major events and what sort of hurdles one may have to face during that year, and how the obstacles could be sorted out.

3. UNION OF BRIDE AND BRIDEGROOM

The Academy tallies the horoscopes of the bride and the bridegroom before marriage. It studies the prospects of their union in marriage. It finds out whether the union will be in the interest of either party, and also what hurdles they are likely to face in their conjugal life.

The full report is made available to the concerned person.

4. DETERMINATION OF AUSPICIOUS TIME

In response to anxious enquiries the Academy works out the *muhurt* or auspicious time one wants to know to begin any job. One may want to know the auspicious time to set up business, lay the foundation stone of a new house, enter the newly-built or allotted house and solemnise marriage or sacred-thread ceremony.

The Academy finds out the time and informs the correspondent.

5. EXTRA-MURAL SERVICES

This department undertakes to do all such jobs which are of a special kind. The department assures fullest confidence to the correspondents. Individual inquiries are attended to in confidence.

The department also undertakes to conduct the chanting of the appropriate *mantra* for the deserving individual. It undertakes to organise *yajnas* too including Vedic ceremonies, rituals and rites.

LIFE GIVING INSTRUMENTS

The Academy has over years perfected in the making of certain life giving instruments. It has built an extensive network to supply the instruments to desirous persons. The following instruments are available:

1. SHRI YANTRA

It is a prestigious instrument made out of metals. It has been energised with Vedic *mantras*. It is particularly helpful for business prosperity and economic progress. It is considered auspicious to place this instrument in the foundation of the building being raised. It could be located in the oratory or in business premises.

2. KANAKA DHARA YANTRA

This instrument is very glorious in itself. Indian sages of yore had acclaimed it. It has, therefore, a long heritage in India. It is particularly helpful for business prosperity and in all other walks of life. It has already proved its efficacy in ensuring business prosperity, jumps in service, economic progress, removal of hurdles, restoration of peace at home and integrity of the family life. It is also metallic, energised with tested Vedic *mantras*.

3. VIJAYA GANAPATI

The Vijaya Ganapati idol is made out of metals. It is also energised with tested Vedic *mantras*.

According to the hoary Indian practices the first God one worships at home is Ganapati and the first God one sets up at home is, again, Ganapati. It is considered to be highly auspicious.

The Academy has, therefore, pooled up all its resources to forge an appropriate idol, which is auspicious from all angles.

It is, generally, acknowledged that one can have great and auspicious advancement in one's life if the idol is set up in one's home or business premises.

4. BAGALAMUKHI YANTRA

This instrument is made of silver. It is also energised with tested Vedic *mantras*. It is particularly effective in overcoming the enemy. It also helps in law suits, electoral success and also in reaping benefits in business competition.

It gives total security against state terror and state authoritarianism. It has been found to be very effective. Its impact has been found to be enduring.

5. BHAGYODAYA YANTRA

This instrument is also made of silver. It is also energised with tested Vedic *mantras*. This instrument has been found to be particularly effective in prevailing over all kinds of obstacles and difficulties besetting the individual's life and progress. It is true we are always confronted with all kinds of troubles and hurdles. The person whose horoscope or palm is vitiated by adverse planetary confluences or obstacle lines will find in it the only relief ensuring their victory over difficulties and hurdles.

6. ASHTALAKSHMI YANTRA

This instrument has been found to be very effective in ensuring economic progress and brisk financial advancement. In fact, it ensures all material comforts and accomplishments.

There are some persons whose horoscopes or palms indicate certain eclipse in their prosperity. For such persons this instrument has been particularly helpful.

OTHER ATTRACTIONS

The Academy has launched its own publications. It publishes only rare and special volumes. Some of the publications such as *Mantra Rahasya, Sammohan Vidya* and *Vrihad Tantra Sadhana* have been highly commended by scholars of repute.

To conclude we hold that hypnotism has the inherent quality to ensure mankind remarkable success. We believe the present volume is but a small contribution to the well-merited efforts to reach hypnotism to all corners of the world.

The facts given in this volume have stood the tests of practicability verification and proof. If the upcoming generation derives benefits from this volume, it will be deemed to be a big step towards social harmony and individual integrity.

Without accepting any aid or assistance the Academy has been involved in all these services. In the coming 10 years the Academy, it is hoped, will be able to put in more efforts and achieve lasting accomplishments.

Persons interested in the activities of the Academy may address their inquiries to:

The Secretary

Bharatiya Jyotish Adhyayan Anusandhan Kendra

(Centre for the Study and Research in Indian Astrological Sciences)
Dr. Shrimali Road, High Court Colony, Jodhpur–342001, Rajasthan, INDIA
Telephone: (0291) 2432209, 2433623

www.ingramcontent.com/pod-product-compliance
Lightning Source LLC
Chambersburg PA
CBHW070839030726
47504CB00005B/1155

* 9 7 8 9 3 8 1 3 8 4 4 6 6 *